Praise for *Love Me Tender*

'*Love Me Tender* is a book unlike any other. It's a page-turner that tumbles forth like a horror story, albeit one punctuated by sex, swimming, injustice and love. Committed to truth-telling, no matter how rough, but also intriguingly suspended in a cloud of unknowing and pain, *Love Me Tender* is a wry, original, agonising book destined to become a classic of its kind' Maggie Nelson, author of *On Freedom*

'What remains when a person shears away – like sacrificing her gorgeous locks – the family, the "good breeding," the "brilliant career" and every pleasing role she was meant to play? In the case of Constance Debré, what remains is a deadpan, tensile thread of a voice: calm, Camusian, comic, stark, relentless and totally hypnotic' Rachel Kushner, author of *The Hard Crowd*

'Direct, propulsive and surpassingly honest. Her chronicle of day-to-day existence during a period of familial upheaval and sexual exploration is one in which every detail is rendered interesting, every episode surprising, by the author's uncanny ability to make understatement sparkle' Gary Indiana, author of *Tiny Fish That Only Want to Kiss*

'*Love Me Tender* is written with edge and urgency in a voice that is both vulnerable and in full command. I read it in one sitting and was taken over by its narrative energy and shocked by the story it tells' Colm Tóibín, author of *The Magician*

'Intense … a character striving mightily for authenticity and honesty, questioning and rending the veil of social norms, acknowledging the Absurd, in hopes of finding some more solid, albeit subjective, truth' Claire Messud, author of *Kant's Little Prussian Head and Other Reasons Why I Write*

'In cruel, brilliant sentences that tighten around the truth like teeth, a fierce character emerges; a new kind of rebel in a queer masterpiece' Holly Pester, author of *Comic Timing*

'*Love Me Tender* is a spitting, snarling tour de force of fuck-you feminist defiance. Pulling us straight from the tender moments of a mother meeting her estranged child, right into a whirlwind of lesbian pick-ups, Parisian apartment-hopping and chain smoking, Debré's novel is a stark reminder of society's suspicion towards women – particularly mothers – who resist easy definition. Wry, bold and confronting, *Love Me Tender* insists on a woman's right to define herself, to choose her own life' Imogen Crimp, author of *A Very Nice Girl*

LOVE ME TENDER

Constance Debré

Translated by Holly James

TUSKAR ROCK PRESS

First published in Great Britain in 2023 by
Tuskar Rock Press
an imprint of Profile Books Ltd
29 Cloth Fair
London
EC1A 7JQ
www.profilebooks.com

By arrangement with Semiotext(e), Los Angeles

First published in the United States of America in 2022 by Semiotext(e), Los Angeles

Original French edition published in France in 2020 by Flammarion, Paris

Copyright © Semiotext(e), 2022
Translated by Holly James

This work received support from the Cultural Services of the French Embassy in the United States through their publishing assistance program.

Special thanks to Kim Calder, Juliana Halpert, and Alice Tassel.

Layout: Hedi El Kholti

10 9 8 7 6 5 4 3 2 1

Printed and bound in Great Britain by Clays Ltd, Elcograf S.p.A.

The moral right of the author has been asserted.

A CIP catalogue record for this book is available from the British Library.

ISBN 978 1 80081 483 7
eISBN 978 1 80081 485 1

FSC
www.fsc.org
MIX
Paper from
responsible sources
FSC® C018072

"There can be a father without a mother"
— Aeschylus, *Oresteia*

I don't see why the love between a mother and son should be any different from other kinds of love. Why we shouldn't be allowed to stop loving each other. Why we shouldn't be allowed to break up. I don't see why we shouldn't stop giving a shit, once and for all, about love, or so-called love, love in all its forms, even that one. I don't see why we absolutely have to love each other, in families or elsewhere, and why we have to go on about it the whole time, to ourselves, to each other. I wonder whose idea it was, when it came about, whether it's a trend, a form of neurosis, compulsion, madness. I wonder what the economic interests are, the political motives. I wonder what they're hiding from us, what they're trying to get out of us with all this talk about love. I look around me and all I see are lies, all I see is madness. When are we going to stop? Why shouldn't we? I need to know. I've been asking myself the question.

I go swimming every day, I have a muscular back and shoulders, I have short hair that's brown with a bit of gray at the front, I have part of a Caravaggio tattooed on my left arm and delicate lettering on my stomach that says Son of a Bitch, I'm tall and slim, I have small breasts, I have a ring in my right ear, I wear jeans, canvas pants, black or white T-shirts, men's shirts in summer, an old leather jacket and Converse or Church's, I don't wear a bra, I sleep in men's gray Oxford boxers, I don't wear makeup, I brush my teeth three times a day, I don't use deodorant, I don't sweat a lot but sometimes I like to, the cologne I wear is called Habit Rouge, sometimes I feel like switching to something else but the girls like it, so I stick with it, I also smell of chlorine, what with all the swimming, I smoke Marlboro lights in the evening, I don't drink a lot, I don't take drugs, I live in Paris in a studio near Denfert Rochereau, I don't have any furniture apart from a double mattress I got from a discount store on rue Saint Maur and a plank of wood with trestles, 17.90 euro the set from Bricorama on Avenue Flandre, I don't like stuff, I don't have any pans, cutlery, or plates apart from a few disposable ones, so I don't have to do any washing up, I don't have any money because I don't give a shit, I'd rather write than work, I don't feel 47, I guess I'll wake up one day and suddenly be old, unless I die before then, like my mother did, apart from the fact that I don't see my son anymore, everything's going well, he's eight, my son, then he'll be nine, then ten, then eleven, his name is Paul, he's great.

I

1

Three years ago. We're at the Flore, sitting outside, Rue Saint-Benoît. It's summer. I'm dipping my black pepper potato chips in some ketchup. I've ordered a club sandwich, he's having a croque monsieur. He's my ex. The first man I was with, and until further notice, the last. We're actually still married because we never got a divorce. We lasted twenty years, he and I. It's been three years since I left him. His name is Laurent. With our eight-year-old son, with Paul, we do alternate weeks, all civil, we've never had any problems. A few months ago I switched to girls. That's what I want to tell him. That's the point of this dinner. I picked the Flore out of habit. We met here when we were twenty, it became one of our haunts. I still live in the 6th, I grew up here, I've never really lived anywhere else. But I don't go to the Flore anymore. I quit my job as a lawyer, I'm writing a book, I've got the tax people on my back and no cash to my name. It's a pain, obviously, but it's not important. So I spit it out, I say, I've started seeing girls. Just in case there was any doubt in his mind, with the new short hair, the new tattoos, the look in general. It's basically the same as before, obviously just a bit more distinct. It's not as if he never had his doubts. We had a little chat about it, a good ten years ago. I said, Nope, no idea what you're talking about. I mean I'm dating girls, I say to him now. Fucking girls would be more accurate. He says, All I want is for you to be happy. This sounds like a lie but it suits me fine, I don't reply. He's barely touched his croque monsieur, he lights a cigarette, calls the waiter over, orders more champagne. That's what he's drinking these days, he says it agrees with him, that it makes him feel less shitty in the morning. The check comes, he pays, we leave. Instead of going his own way on Boulevard Saint-Germain, he walks me towards the Seine. When we get to my door, he goes to follow me upstairs, as if we hadn't been separated for three years, as if I hadn't just told him what I just told him. I say no, he says, Have it your way.

The next day he messages me, Yesterday was nice what are you doing tonight? I thought we'd settled things but maybe he's thought about it and wants to talk some more. We've hardly seen each other in three years, I liked it just fine that way. But I agree to meet him, I tell myself I probably owe him that much. He comes to pick me up outside my house in a taxi, it looks like he's made an effort, he's made reservations at a restaurant in another district, a fairly chic place in the courtyard of an *hôtel particulier*. He talks to the waiters like a regular, he orders a good wine like a connoisseur, he acts like some guy trying to impress his girlfriend. Maybe this is what he does now with girls, maybe he wants to show me, try out his techniques. He wanted to meet but he's not saying anything, he's not asking any questions, not a word about yesterday, nothing about him or me, we talk about holidays, foreign countries, books we've read, as though we're politely humoring each other on a date that's not going anywhere. He wants us to walk home together, I make sure there's enough space between our bodies, not too close, not too far, as if everything were normal. The Marais, the Seine, Notre-Dame, we're like a Chinese couple on honeymoon. Once again he walks me right to my door, once again he wants to come up with me, to kiss me, once again he seems surprised when I say no.

In October, I bring up the subject of divorce. There's a girl I've been seeing since summer. She's young, she doesn't like the fact that I'm married. She's been on my case, she keeps making scenes, in the end I give in. And she's right, it isn't healthy, I call him my ex, he still calls me his wife. I invite Laurent for coffee, one day, then another day, he says he doesn't have time, he's avoiding me. In the end I send him an email. I want to get divorced, it'd make things clearer for everyone, come over for dinner one night and we can talk, take care. Stop you're turning me on. That's his reply, which he sends in an email. In the moment, I find it funny. A little crazy, but funny.

Fifteen days later, around Halloween, he tells me something's up with Paul. He says he's keeping him there, that there's no need for me to pick him up. He says Paul can't stand me, that he's rolling around on the floor, that he hates me. I go over. My son is rolling around on the floor. He hates me.

At this point, I don't make any connection between the facts, between the father and the son. Maybe Laurent's right, maybe Paul does hate me, maybe it is my fault, maybe I have done something wrong. I try to understand what I've done, what I've failed to do. I haven't been giving him as much attention recently, I have to admit. I've been there the whole time but I've been a little distracted. I've been writing my book. You don't have space for anyone when you're writing. And then there were the girls. At first, I didn't say anything to him. But in the end, we had a chat. Not right away, not about the first girl, nor the second, but the third girl he met in passing, he liked her. He said, Why don't we go on holiday with her, that would be nice. But we'd just broken up, I told him we couldn't, I explained. I asked him whether he already suspected something, whether it bothered him. He already suspected something, it didn't bother him. We went out, he took my hand, we went to get a soda at la Palette downstairs, we were both in a good mood, we often were, come to think of it. We carried on as before. There were the weeks where he stayed with me and I took care of him, then there were the weeks where he stayed with his dad, and I took care of the girls. I was always careful. Everything was going well. I know it was. Some things you just know.

Since November, Paul's been staying with his dad, I don't see him anymore, I don't speak to him anymore. Every time I propose something, Laurent either refuses or doesn't reply. Nothing, no news, not a word. The weeks go by, then the weeks turn into months. I don't threaten to take him to court, I don't want to make things worse. One day, when I'm feeling fed up, more so than usual, I go over to his, to theirs. Laurent opens up, doesn't say a word, goes into the living room. Paul's in his bed, duvet pulled over his head, head on the pillow. Laurent's in the next room, smoking. I speak to Paul but he doesn't move, doesn't look at me, doesn't answer me. I try different tones of voice, I ask him how he is, I try to make him laugh, I talk about something else, I ask him what this is all about, I say, Come on, come and get a Coke downstairs with me, he doesn't open his eyes, he doesn't move a muscle, he's tense, stubborn, heavy as lead. Finally I lose my temper, I yell at him, That's enough now, get up, get dressed, come with me just for five minutes. He gets out of bed, he goes to his dad in the living room, he hides behind him, he's shaking and yelling, he tells me to go to hell, he gives me the finger. Laurent points at the door and yells, Now get out. I look at him and realize he's stronger, physically stronger than me, the fact that we're the same height, that we wear the same clothes, that we occupy space in the same way, that we speak at the same volume, none of that makes any difference. That's when I realize that the difference between a man and a woman is just a question of weight and muscles. I look at Laurent and see he's thinking the same thing, I look at Paul standing behind his dad and see there's nothing I can do, I tell myself this is between them, their little guy thing, I shrug my shoulders, I leave.

At the local dive bar run by the Chinese family, I tell my friends from the swimming pool what happened. Dominique and Ming say, That's crazy, you have to do something, speak to Laurent's parents, go to the police, André says, Leave it, it'll be all right, your son will come round sooner or later. He says something similar happened with his daughter after his own separation. It all worked out in the end.

Fall comes and goes, then winter, then spring. The whole time I wait for things to settle, I figure they'll get tired eventually, I try to speak to Laurent, try to see Paul. There's no getting through, it's the Berlin Wall. I haven't seen Paul for six months. A friend of mine, a family lawyer, offers to help me. For free, seeing as I'm broke. When summer comes around, he files for divorce on my behalf with a request for urgent measures to be granted so I can see Paul every other week, just as before. I say to myself, worst-case scenario, I'll have him for half the school vacation and on weekends, just like any dad who walks out on his family.

The hearing is set for the end of July. One year after the episode at the Flore. Two days before the hearing, I receive Laurent's written submissions, signed by his lawyer. He's applying for sole custody with termination of my parental rights. He's accusing me of incest and pedophilia, committed against my eight-year-old son, directly or through involvement of a third party. He's written about my homosexual friends "who may or may not be pedophiles." He's included a picture of my son sitting outside on a terrace with one of my fag friends the day we went to get a soda together, a photo of a sign that reads "Danger! Hunting," found in a field and kept on my desk, near Paul's bedroom door. He's quoted passages from books selected from my bookshelves, Bataille, Duvert, Guibert. He's putting everything together, making his case, sowing doubt. My nine-year-old son has written a letter to the court saying that living with me is inhumane, that his dad says I'm insane, and he agrees. He says he doesn't want to see me anymore.

The hearing lasts fifteen minutes, Laurent's lawyer reads passages from *Crazy for Vincent*, as if I were Hervé Guibert's narrator, as if Paul were the young boy he sleeps with in the book, the judge stares at the tattoo poking out from beneath my sleeve, she asks me why I'm writing a book and what it's about, she wants to know why I speak to my son about my homosexuality, she says that these subjects are not appropriate for children, that it's not a question of legality, it's a question of morals, she's sure I can understand, I am, after all, an intelligent woman.

The judge's ruling is issued a few days later. She's appointed a psychiatrist to examine all three of us. She's giving him six months to hand in his report. As always when it comes to legal matters, the timeframe is just a guideline. It could take a year, two years, three years. In the meantime, Laurent has been granted sole custody. I have only limited, supervised visitation rights, according to the ruling. One hour every fifteen days at an association, a "meeting space" near République, where pedagogical experts will monitor meetings between me and Paul, just like they do for some (but not all) moms on crack or dads who beat their kids. "Unless the parties agree otherwise," it says. "Until we have a clearer understanding of the situation," explains Madame C., Family Judge at the Judicial Court of Paris. I appeal, but it doesn't halt the proceedings. The decision and its provisional enforcement still apply. There won't be a hearing for two years. Two years might as well be a thousand years. Two years might as well be never.

2

If you were to commit a crime, what would it be? That's what my colleagues and I used to ask each other when I was a lawyer. You had to choose a crime that would say something about you, one with some kind of meaning. But the rule was that you could only choose one. Marie went for assassination with a handgun. I was quite taken with the idea of gambling fraud, rigged matches, that kind of thing, but for me there was nothing quite like a seamlessly executed hold-up, hands in the air, cash in the bag, get in the car and go.

Incest had never occurred to me. It's such a rich crime, the basis of so many things, in mythology, in psychoanalysis, in literature, it's the foundation, the order of the world, of families, of civilization, the great taboo. It's got quite a ring to it, incest. A real man's crime. Almost a mark

(21)

of recognition for a woman. I guess I'm hunting on their territory. I guess they can't stand to see me get hard. But it's too great an honor for me, Your Grace. It's girls I'm interested in. Girls of age, generally. I like them experienced.

First there was Socrates, then Jesus, then Oscar Wilde, and now me. We're a select few. And while I'm at it, there was also Spinoza: "Cursed be he by day and cursed be he by night; cursed be he when he lies down and cursed be he when he rises up; The Lord will not spare him." You just don't get that kind of writing from the Judicial Court of Paris these days. No great life is complete without a trial, you have to ruffle a few feathers, you can't just be a good little child all your life.

I went to pick up the ruling myself. It was August 4th. A bad omen, I said to myself, like Malesherbes tripping up on his way to the gallows. My lawyer was on vacation in Mexico. He'd been sending me pictures of Inca temples. It was really hot. I crossed the Seine on my scooter. The courts were deserted. It was the old Palais de Justice, the one next to Sainte-Chapelle. I already knew the building like the back of my hand, the criminal trials court, the examining magistrate's gallery, the anti-terrorism wing, immediate summons, it was like coming home. I spent years here defending rapists, thieves, armed robbers, pedophiles, con artists, murderers. But the family court was uncharted territory. I never took on divorces. They were too nasty for me.

The clerk prints out the document. She hands it to me. I read it in front of her. I'm careful not to change my expression. I fold the piece of paper into quarters. I slip it into my jacket pocket. Thank you madame, goodbye madame. I put my sunglasses back on. I walk back through the Palais de Justice. I don't see any of my lawyer friends or anyone else I know, everyone's on vacation. I concentrate on my breathing, on each gesture, I move slowly. I get on the scooter. I cross the Seine. I park in front of La Palette, rest the scooter on its stand, turn the engine off, take off my helmet and lock it away under the seat. I take a few steps and sit down on the curb. Five minutes pass, maybe ten, I don't know. I get up again. I walk home, I pass the fob over the sensor, I push the door open with my shoulder, I go up the five flights of stairs, I put the key in the lock, I enter the one-bedroom apartment I've been living in for three years, the place I moved to when I left Laurent. There's one bedroom for Paul and I sleep on the couch in the living room. I won't be needing this place anymore, I won't be needing a bed for him, I don't need all these things, all his stuff, all mine. In any case I've stopped paying rent. Time to get rid. Time to get out. What else can I do but keep going, speed up, carry on living like a young man, a single bachelor. A solitary man, as Johnny Cash says. From now on I'm a lonesome cowboy.

3

Number one has hairs that go all the way down her thighs and up her stomach, a black, downy trail up to her navel, smooth, brown skin, nice shoulders, beautiful legs. I mostly touch her with my hand, the tips of my fingers, my palm, my thumb. I don't really go down on her, it's not something she's particularly comfortable with yet, and I'm not either, to be honest, not with her, I think it's the hair. She says she's not a lesbian, but with me it's different. She's petite but chubby, her stomach her ass her thighs, the way some children are, the way adolescence sometimes clings beneath the skin. She lives in an apartment with her sister on the same floor as their parents on Boulevard Voltaire. In November she's moving to a studio on the fifth floor. She has the same name as one of the previous girls, which is a shame for the list. I give her a number.

Number two is slim, about my age, she has pale skin but you can tell she'll tan in the summer, she has small breasts, I haven't touched them yet, I haven't seen her naked yet, I only put my hand on her back, on her neck, the day I saw her after announcing that I didn't want us to see each other anymore, she started to cry, I started to cave, her hair's fairly short, a little curly, very fine, it's light brown, almost blond with a few grays mixed in. I haven't seen her apartment yet, she lives just north of the Luxembourg Gardens, she has two daughters and a suede jacket, she told me she's straight as well, I'll probably sleep with her on Sunday.

I met them both in the same week, in the same café just below my flat, La Palette. It was the week I moved out. I left my 430ft² apartment for 100ft² in the fifth. I was broke, I didn't have a credit card, I was making a bit of cash by selling all my books at Gibert Jeune, rummaging through the bins for macarons at Ladurée on rue Jacob at six in the morning before going swimming. I was getting by. I didn't go anywhere, I was writing my book, I didn't give a shit about anything else. Even with a gun to my head I wouldn't have done anything differently. By the time I moved out, the book was finished. And I'm never going back to my life as a lawyer. That, at least, is finito, forever.

Each day I'd take more of my books, clothes and furniture outside. I left everything out on the street. I didn't even need to have a removal company come and pick it up, I watched it all disappear from my window, it was amazing, the little ants of the 6th dissecting it all, collecting it all up. At first, I didn't think I could get rid of the books, Homer, Baudelaire, Musil, Duras, you don't dare throw them away. Then you realize you can, of course you can, nothing happens, they're just things. I threw everything out. Everything but two bags that I took on the back of my scooter when I left. And Paul's things. I put them in boxes and put the boxes in my friends' basement, I guess they'll go moldy.

They were the ones hitting on me. The girls. Now I'm a lesbian it's always the same. They must be able to see from a mile off that I'm up for it. In the beginning, I was looking for love. But it's not about that anymore. The closer I get, the further away I feel. And the easier it gets. Girls don't weigh you down.

They're nothing like each other in terms of age, appearance, language, tastes. Two completely different models. One blond one brunette, one old one young, one thin one fat, one shaven one hairy, one left bank one right bank. They could have made up a whole, each one a distraction from the other. But that's not how it works.

When she's turned on, the young one takes my hand and slides it towards her cunt for me to put my fingers inside her. She says she loves it when I'm behind her, my hips pressing against her body. She says that sexuality has always been complicated for her, something she's been thinking about for a long time. She says she doesn't know how to touch me. She tried once, I said, Let's leave it for some other time. The other day I asked her to get herself off, she lay on her stomach, slid both hands between her thighs and started moving back and forth, touching herself, her ass moving up and down, I don't really know when she came.

I took the first apartment I could find, 500 euros for 100ft^2 just behind the Pantheon. There's a little square downstairs, a few cafes, students everywhere, a kebab shop called With Or Without Fries, a Lebanese restaurant opposite that sells chicken kebab for 4.90 euro, the swimming pool isn't far, I have a fridge that I have to unplug at night because of the noise, a plastic plant on the windowsill, a mattress on wooden slats, two drawers, a shower in the corner of the room, a laundromat just downstairs, the place gets no natural light in the day but there's a bright light coming from a spotlight just beneath the window at night, the phone doesn't work, it's a bit like a cave, I'm stealing WiFi from the neighbors. 100ft^2 is the size of a prison cell or a monk's cell. It's very Ignatius of Loyola, very spiritual retreat. There's a certain joy that comes from doing things you didn't think yourself capable of.

I'm two streets away from the last apartment I lived in with Laurent. Paul was a year old when we moved to rue Descartes and five when we each went our own way and split him in two. It was in that apartment that he learned to walk, talk, and do all those other things that parents generally find so moving. The place had crooked floorboards and a threadbare carpet, we'd light fires in the fireplace, there was a little garden downstairs, I'd park the Peugeot in the car park opposite, bump into Inès de La Fressange in the elevator. I'm also two streets away from Lycée Henri IV, where I spent my last years of high school, dying of boredom. I guess the school should remind me of my first life, the one that came to an end when my mother died one morning in September, the year before I finished high school, because of drugs. I guess the windows on rue Descartes should bring back memories of my second life, my family life, my life as a straight person, before I took an automatic rifle to it. I guess these things should make me feel nostalgia, sadness, regret. But no, nothing.

I still have the same legs, same ears, same arms as I did then, but everything else has changed. For three years now, whole parts of me have been crumbling away. And it keeps on happening. Just when I think I'm getting somewhere, I turn around and I'm living a different life, I'm a different me. It all blends into one, all those things I threw out the window, the stuff, the job, the money, the family. Then there's the things that are happening now, the things that are finally happening to me. It saps your energy, of course, spending years like this, all the corpses you end up dragging along behind you. Was Orlando tired by the end of the book? What about the lovers in Only Lovers Left Alive? I can't remember. I'm going gray, which is hardly surprising. But there are plateaus, too. Physically, for example, I've reached a plateau. No new tattoos, no new piercings, regular exercise, same haircut, short but not shaved, same style of clothes, boys' clothes that any girl can wear too, as simple and plain as possible, black, white, and gray, nothing to bog me down, a style inspired by emptiness, the only one for me. The sex hasn't changed either, licking, fingering, ass fucking, all very nice and polite, I get what I give, more or less. A learning plateau. One thing that has been changing is my mentality. Before, I wanted everything to go smoothly, now I've realized that nobody owes anybody anything.

It's the tipping point, the Kairos, it's like the conversion of Saint Augustine, just as radical. It's not just a matter of him believing in God or me liking women, it's the fact that there's a life before and a life after. For me, homosexuality isn't about who I'm fucking, it's about who I become. With men there was always a limit, now I have all the space I want, I feel like I can do anything. Women, love, sex, in the beginning it was all new and exciting, but not anymore. It's all still there, of course, it's still the subject matter of what's happening to me, but it's not important, like the décor of a room, I have to go beyond that to find what I'm looking for. For me, homosexuality just means taking a break from everything. That's exactly what it is, a long vacation, expansive as the sea with nothing on the horizon, nothing to close it, nothing to define it. That's why I quit my job. To be both the master and the slave, the only one responsible for setting the limits. Work, family, apartments, finito. And you can't imagine how good it feels.

I meet up with the skinny one, 6 o'clock, Place de l'Odéon. It's still nice out. She's drawing when I arrive, then she closes her sketchbook. We talk for a while. We kiss. Not too long, not too hard, she's looking at me with her green eyes. I order a barley water. She says, Did you know your tongue tastes sweet, but your lips don't? She slides her hand underneath my worn denim jacket, ripped at the shoulder, she strokes my skin, runs her hand over my breasts, grazing my nipples.

"Are you going to come to mine?"
"When?"
"Tomorrow, the day after, the day after that."

She's wearing a dress, I run my hand over her slim legs, under the table, all the way from the top to the bottom, her legs are cleanly shaven.

The other one, the young one, has a leather couch, a bunch of old CDs, piles of clothes everywhere, a multi-colored duvet, cheap toiletries in the bathroom, shower gels and spray deodorants. In the morning I go into the kitchen. I make toast and Nespresso coffee. I help myself to mango juice, honey and butter. I leave early. I don't bump into her sister or parents on the way out.

The skinny one comes over on Friday. We sit on my bed, we kiss, she undresses me really quickly and then goes down on me. Not bad for a first time, I think, I fuck her then we go to hers on my scooter, she has a big apartment, pretty nice, her bedroom walls are gray, she makes maca-roni and we put some vinyls on, Depeche Mode and something by Tom Waits I've never heard before, we fuck again then fall asleep, her two cats jump on the bed all night, scratching my feet. In the morning she makes tea, we fuck again, we read books. She has Aesop products, I take a bath and then she buys me lunch on rue Grégoire-de-Tours, I drink a glass of wine.

Sometimes, they come over to mine. They text me when they arrive and I go down to open the door, I haven't given them the code to get into the building, we fuck in the single bed. More often than not, I go to theirs, to number one's studio on Boulevard Voltaire above her parents' apartment, to number two's big apartment on rue de Tournon when she doesn't have her daughter. I often sleep over, I alternate between breakfasts, Chocapic with one, smoked tea with the other. I read in their beds, take baths in their bathtubs, take stuff from their fridges. I take what they have to give, I watch what happens when I touch them. I call them both honey. It would be nice to be able to pay them to avoid any misunderstandings.

4

My work consists of waiting, swimming, and fucking girls.

Waiting for the book to come out, waiting for the court case to start moving, waiting for a bit of cash to come through, waiting to see my son again. Waiting for things to calm down, for the universe to adjust, to heal, to rebuild itself. My universe. I won't go back, I won't climb back into my old skin.

No way.

If I'd have settled for just liking women, it would've been fine, I think. Lesbian lawyer, same life, same income, same appearance, same opinions, same ideals, same relationship to work, money, love, family, society, the material world, the body. If I still had the same relationship to the

(33)

world, it would've been much less hassle. But that wasn't an option, that's not how it works, I didn't go through all this just for more of the same. I did it for a new life, for the adventure. I think that's what makes them so mad, Laurent, the judges, all the people who don't speak to me anymore. As if they'd never felt it themselves, the temptation to just chuck it all in. As if it were that big a deal, as if they were the ones stealing food from Franprix, walking a tightrope.

I might have given up everything but I'm not doing anything out of the ordinary. I go to bed early, I get up early, I don't drink, I don't take drugs, I don't spend my Sunday afternoons doing BDSM, I'm not fighting any battles, I'm not part of any community, I don't have any particular affinities. Swimming, reading, writing, and seeing girls, like an ascetic. If it weren't for the cigarettes and the sex, I'd be practically straight edge, hardcore in my own way. Of course it'd be total anarchy if everyone lived like I do. I'll pay for it, there's no doubt about it, just give me the check, *la cuenta por favor*, no problemo, you always have to pay in the end.

In any case, waiting is all you can do when fate is crushing your face into the ground with its shoe. You can't move. There's no point even trying. That's when you have to be strong. You have to do a bit of scheming for cash, ten euros here and there, to keep a roof over your head, to be able to buy cigarettes, scheming for all kinds of things, to get through the day, to be able to sleep at the end of it. That's what separates the ones who survive from the ones who crumble, the ones who throw themselves in the Seine, hit the bottle, start popping Xanax, end up in the hospital, out on the streets, in jail.

I get it. I've always been able to understand them, the ones who just can't do it. But I can. I think there's something in my body keeping me going. At least that's what it feels like, seeing as I never made any active decision to keep going. There's something ticking over in my brain, or maybe some kind of chemistry, I don't know. All I know is that I don't feel anything anymore. I could walk on glass. It could break at any moment, of course. I have to be careful. Very careful. If my skin gives up on me, I have nothing. That's why I swim. To keep my body in balance, to keep my body strong. Because that's what's holding me together. Because there's something in my muscles that's connected to my soul. I know that if I don't go swimming, I end up having a bad day. I'm running on empty, I can't afford even the slightest detour. So I swim every day, I don't even think about it anymore. I do it, and that's that. It's my form of discipline, my method, my own form of madness to keep the madness at bay. I cut up time, reduce everything to simple gestures, then carry them out.

I alternate between swimming pools: Taris, Pontoise, Saint-Germain, Les Halles, Butte-aux-Cailles, Joséphine Baker. Head in the water. Forty minutes. Front crawl for two kilometers. It's my contract with myself. My only commitment. It's a question of life or death. The day I stop will be the day I fall apart. I always feel better after my shower. I only take showers at the pool now. There's a lot of space. A friendly atmosphere. I'm in pretty good shape thanks to all the swimming. Just by the by. It's important to look good. To look good and be strong. Otherwise I would have blown my brains out long ago. Each day I save myself. Then I do it all over again the next day.

And then there's the girls. Just the two of them that fall. But it was good. It was necessary. All the time I spent with them was vital. I needed to make sure I was still alive. I don't see what you can do when you feel depressed other than engage in small talk with someone you don't know. Sex helps you unwind. Plus it's free, like going to Mass. I also go to church, incidentally. I light a candle and ask forgiveness for my sins.

What do you think about when you swim? Nothing. I don't think about anything. And apart from Mass or AC/DC, I don't listen to anything, either. Do you really not give a shit about other people? That's what G. asked me, much later, when I was about to kiss her. As if I'd had time to think about it. I dodged the question. People don't get it. Just now in church, Saint-Germain-des-Prés, I saw an ex-voto that said This Is My Beloved Son In All His Splendor Listen To Him. I took a photo. My work consists of waiting, swimming, and fucking girls. *Agnus dei qui tollis peccata mundi.*

5

The ruling was issued in August. At the beginning of September I wrote to Laurent to ask if I could see Paul. My right to an hour-long visit every fifteen days at the association, supervised by the pedagogical experts, as authorized by the High Court of Paris, was "unless the parties agree otherwise." There were no available slots at the association anyway. They were already snowed under by all the other families whose business the state was sticking its nose into. Every week I called, every week they told me there were no slots for months. I asked Laurent if I could see Paul in a public place or in the house of a "trusted third party," I suggested cafes, restaurants, the Luxembourg Gardens, meeting him on the walk to school, going to McDonalds, the little Chinese restaurant on rue de Buci, the Japanese on rue Mazet, La Palette, the cafe by the town hall, Le Flore, Saint Sulpice square, a quasi-aristocratic aunt on rue Bonaparte, my dad's place in the countryside, friends in the 9th, the 6th, the 14th, the 20th. I wanted to see him just to see him, I wanted to see him so I could tell him that it was OK, that it was going to be OK, that there was no harm done, that we would get through this. Laurent refused everything. More often than not he didn't even reply. No news from Paul, no news about him. I told myself he must be OK, otherwise I would know. That period lasted nine months, like a pregnancy but the wrong way around. A birth in reverse.

6

I break up with the young one, I stop by a party in a club,
I'm meeting some friends there, and suddenly she turns
up. She follows me to the toilets, I'm washing my hands,
I look in the mirror, I say, What the hell are you doing
here? Just once a week, she says, I tell her it's over, I don't
want to see her anymore, she's drunk, I'm tired, I'm starting
to get a migraine, that's the problem for me, the lack of
sleep, the tiredness, I head to the cloakroom with my
ticket, she says she's leaving with me, she won't leave me
alone, my friends are watching, they feel sorry for me, it
happens to everyone at some point, this kind of situation,
she follows me down the street, I say, I'll call you a taxi,
she says no, she wants to walk with me, she carries on
walking, talking, I have a headache, I want to sleep, she
wants to come back to my 100ft^2 apartment, she says, Tell
me you don't want me anymore, tell me you don't want

my ass, my cunt, I think you're in love with me, I think you really like me, she's crying, yelling, she says I look really beautiful tonight, that's the fucking annoying thing, she says I should never have come here, that the only reason I came was to make out with her, she cries some more, we're somewhere around Saint-Michel when she finally leaves.

The skinny one took me to a party on Saturday. It was in a kind of office space in the 10th. A start-up. We don't have a single Facebook friend in common, we don't know any of the same people, this never happens in Paris. It was cold, we came from hers on my scooter, she's light, I like the feeling of having her there behind me. There was a big kitchen with a blackboard where everyone's supposed to write nice things. The people there were all her age, which is to say my age, they seemed older, that's often the case with straight people, they asked me what I do for a living, I put some nitrogen in the glass of Côtes du Rhône I poured myself from the box, it made a cloud of vapor, I looked at my glass, she wanted to dance. We went back to hers. I slept. Not enough.

Some girls have something about them, something they refuse to see. Something about their appearance, the way they walk, their clothes, the way they talk. I'm not talking about butch women, or even women like me, now or before, where it's more obvious, but there's always something there. I don't say anything. I don't tell them, they'd get upset, I don't know why, I think it's a beautiful thing. It's like the fags I'm friends with who think no one can tell. Who don't want anyone to notice. The girls I'm sleeping with don't seem to think about it. They sleep with me without giving it a second thought. They act like it doesn't matter that I'm a woman. As if it didn't say anything about them. As if homosexuality didn't exist. As if it were just love.

Sometimes I love one more than I love the other. Sometimes I love them both. Sometimes I don't love either. Sometimes I break up with them. Either one or the other. Just to make things clear. Then I take them back. They insist. They say they love me. They don't ask for much. Only my mouth my hands my ass. I couldn't sleep next to anyone before. Now I can't sleep alone.

I'm learning that I can love anyone, desire anyone, come with anyone, be bored with anyone, hate anyone, I'm learning that there's a fine line between loving and not loving, I don't see why it's such a big deal, I don't see why it should have to be anything more than that, just love, just desire. Why all the drama? That's what I've been wondering.

I don't talk when I fuck. I never say a word. I don't scream when I come, either. Not what I would class as screaming. I breathe, I sigh, I moan. But words, sentences, I don't do that, or only very rarely. Let alone screaming. I feel like that's not the point. Or maybe that's not what I feel. I just don't do it, that's all. Come to think of it, we don't say much at all in my family. We don't talk about the important things. Not love not money not fucking not sadness not fear. That's why I thought it was strange the other day when my father said my mother died at the right time because she wouldn't have been able to stand growing old. She was my age when she died, my mother. Maybe that's why I've been in a hurry these past few years. I told myself his saying that was a good sign, it would help with his guilt, his grief. The young one, on the other hand, likes to talk. She likes to say she's my little wifey, my little bitch, my little whore, my little slut. Stop it, stop it, I say.

The skinny one takes me to the theater, we take the metro back to her place, her daughters are staying over, we go to get burgers and fries from Le Mabillon, she likes to kiss me in the middle of the street, up against cars, Will you two get a room already? Tonight she asks me if I'm in a hurry or something, she says she wants us to have more time, more space, that we could go away for a few days after Christmas, to Italy or maybe Auvergne, that we might be better off waiting until spring because the house is cold. I don't say anything, there's nothing to say. Before I go, I press my palm against her flat stomach, slide my fingers into her jeans, touch the top of her cunt. I walk home. Rue de Tournon, the railings of Luxembourg gardens, rue

Soufflot, rue Saint-Étienne-du-Mont, it's late, I can't sleep, as always I wake up before sunrise, I'm so tired.

At night I dream of my son, complicated dreams, dreams where I'm trying to see him but I don't know if I'm allowed to, where he's there but he doesn't speak to me, I'm afraid he's going to be mean to me, he doesn't say anything but he's not mean either, he's silent, he looks at me the same way he always does, calm, gentle, quiet, I'm afraid Laurent will come because I don't know if I'm supposed to be there or not, that's what always wakes me up, sometimes I go back to sleep, sometimes I don't. Around 7 o'clock, I go swimming, the dream is washed away in the chlorine, under the neon lights, beneath the showers. The days are OK. In the day I'm good at thinking about something else. Or if I do think about it, I don't know what I think, exactly. I couldn't do everything I'm doing if he were here. If I had to take him to school, pick him up, take him to piano lessons, drama class, swimming, tennis, basketball, birthdays, friends' houses, if I had to talk to the other parents, people at the school, if I had to do the shopping, the cooking, the homework. I'd have to go back to a normal apartment, a normal job, a normal life, I couldn't live the way I am now, I couldn't be myself if he were here, I'd have to go all the way back, it seems so far, it seems impossible. I'd like to let go, move on to something else, forget about him.

7

A man called Paul would be loved in a special kind of way,
I thought. It was love I was thinking about, love for him,
later on in life, when I chose his name. The midwives
asked me what his first name was so they could put it on
the little blue bracelets, I told them, No, wait until he's
born, in five minutes or ten or twenty, for now he doesn't
exist, there's no first name, no son, no mother, we have to
wait, respect the order of things, that's what I explained to
them, naked apart from my hospital gown, one day in
May at the maternity hospital in Port-Royal (I was happy
it was that hospital because of Blaise Pascal), I didn't give
a shit about the little blue bracelets, the name I had in
mind for him was none of their business. He was born, I
saw him for the first time, with his own face, his own
body, his own life, his own death, he didn't really cry,
he just had an unhappy look about him, which I liked, I

realized it really was him, not just some abstract concept, I said his name was Paul. He has his father's last name, but his first name, that was me. That's something that doesn't exist in any other form of love, choosing a name for somebody. A name that will make others love that person, so that one day, they'll leave you. They made the little bracelets, one for him and one for me, they dressed him, they took me back to my room, I was starving, they served me steak, I didn't sleep much that night, he cried a little, I felt intimidated, I held him against me, his head on my collar bone, I walked down the corridor, he felt so light and yet so heavy, I thought about the dogs we had when I was a child, the bitches, I thought about what they used to do, how they took care of their puppies, without it ever seeming ridiculous, without any shame, without losing a part of who they were or giving up anything, how they went back to hunting when the next season began, I thought about how simple it was, how there was no need for doubt, I was going to do it my way, without the absurdity that comes with being a woman, the obscenity that comes with being a mother.

8

I avoid parks, schools, bakeries at half past four in the afternoon, I take detours, I hide away on weekends, I wear sunglasses even when it rains. Before I never used to notice them, I never realized how many there were, children all over the place, all kinds of children, the whole range, the babies, the three- to four-year-olds, six to eight, ten to twelve. It feels as though they've been put there just for me, to taunt me, a trick the gods are playing to make fun of me, to remind me of all the things I'm working hard to forget through discipline, telling me it's all for nothing, my discipline, my lengths at the swimming pool, all the girls I've been seeing. I run from children as though they were cluster bombs, as though they could blow up in my face at any moment, riddling my body with small fragments of sharp metal. I can see them coming a mile off, I keep my distance, always dodging them. But they have the upper hand. They always get me in the end. They take me by surprise. Yesterday it was two boys from the ten to twelve category walking behind me somewhere around Saint-Michel. I didn't see them. I heard them. It was their voices that tore me in two. Their voices weren't exactly like his, it was more the tone, the way they talk to each other, boys of that age. I couldn't stop myself from turning around, from feeling the pain, I might as well have hit myself across the face, I might as well have stabbed myself in the thigh.

9

Not having any money gives a sharp clarity to everything. 100ft^2, two pairs of jeans, three T-shirts, an old leather jacket and my old Rolex, just for a laugh, a single espresso to go, a baguette, a packet of cigarettes, my swimming pool pass. The world is turning into a skeleton without any flesh. I'm getting stronger, more focused. It's important to have limits so you don't lose yourself in the chaos. I've been stealing from Franprix and Bio c' Bon, I don't pay my train fare, I jump the barrier, I've learned to ask my friends for a hundred euros, let them pay for my drinks, thank you friends, there are thousands of things I can do without, the doctor for example (but not cigarettes), I'm living on nothing, learning the techniques, getting through the days. Sometimes I steal to eat, sometimes it's just for the sake of it, for the beauty of the gesture. I'm training myself to be indestructible, I need to know that I am.

It wouldn't be the same if I had a safety net, a family to rely on, an inheritance stashed away somewhere, a piece of something or perhaps someone. But I don't have anything. And I don't really have anyone, either. Apart from my dad, who doesn't have a cent to his name, and a few friends, I don't talk to anyone. The conditions are perfect. I'm doing this for real. That's all that matters. It has to be real. There has to be a risk. That's the only thing that counts. I've seen what happened to my parents, to all the clients I've defended, I know it's a slippery slope. I haven't been wrapped in cotton wool like people always think, because of my family name, or because they're morons making lazy assumptions about things that are none of their business. As if the borders were sealed off, as if violence, death and poverty were non-existent among the bourgeoisie. So yes, walking along the rooftops without a safety net, that's the way I like it. I think this is what I've always wanted. It's the kind of life I imagined as a child, when I'd climb the trees and think about the future. Maybe my lousy romanticism doesn't count for anything. But that's the way it is. A life of convenience, a full fridge, the thought makes me want to die.

After my mother died, I realized the situation had its advantages. Same goes when you don't see your child. Because family is hell. Because it drives you mad. Because in the end, living in such close quarters breeds hatred. I wasn't made for the domestic life. That's usually the reason it doesn't work out with girls. After a few weeks or months, when love descends into couple life, practical matters, after the first hundred days. Sometimes they tell me there's something wrong with me. They say I should see a therapist so I can understand why I'm like this. So I can heal. So I can want a house. So I can sleep at night. So I can stop wanting to leave them.

Because the situation gives me a good excuse to leave them. I say, I know, you're right, it's because of Paul, it's because I'm sad, I don't have the space in my life for love, it's nothing to do with you. It scares them away when I don't cry, when I carry on swimming, when I tell them I've never been interested in taking care of anyone else, when I say I don't know whether I miss him or not because I never miss anyone.

10

This is the women's, some girl said to me in the changing rooms. I am a woman, I said. She looked at me without saying a word. Expressionless. She was trying to get her head around it. She wasn't French, probably Filipina, maybe she'd just arrived in Paris, maybe I was the first woman she'd seen who didn't look the way she'd expect a woman to look. I stood there in front of her, without saying a word, expressionless, all five foot nine of me in my jeans and leather jacket, shoes in hand. We looked at each other. I was almost as shocked as she was. It might have only lasted a second. I could see she didn't understand. I realized I'd forgotten there was something a bit different about me, something a bit strange. Something about who I am, what I've learned to be, what I've chosen to be, the figures from my childhood, too. I grew up in a family where the women were manly, where they hunted, drove and smoked while the men drew and read Rimbaud because they didn't like hunting. It was all very gender fluid, the nobility on my mother's side, bourgeoisie on my father's. Or at least it was on the surface, but that was enough for me, it was a good starting point. I got my first rifle when I was fifteen. It was a present from my mother, a former model who always wore perfume and a full face of make-up. It's about time you learned how to shoot. Driving, of course, was something I already knew how to do.

Obviously if he'd been a girl, I'd have managed, but still, I wouldn't have felt comfortable. With the clothes, with the toys, with myself. I'd have felt like a dishonest role model. What does it mean to be a girl? How should I know? That's why it was always easy with Paul, it always worked out. It was so easy to be myself around him. Often easier than being around other people. I didn't have to pretend. I might never have become a lesbian if I hadn't been his mother first, I might never have dared, I might never have understood.

11

Every time I post on Facebook or Instagram, every time I
like something, every time I comment, I know it could be
used against me. Last summer, Laurent collected several
photos that my friends and I had posted online and used
them as evidence. Photos without any sexual connotations.
Photos without any drugs or alcohol. Photos completely
unrelated to Paul. Anything can be misinterpreted, taken
out of context, made to seem more serious than intended.
Even Proust. Just think of Sodom and Gomorrah. Out on
the streets it's all #MeToo and gay marriage, but it's all talk.
In reality, a judge is essentially forcing a mother to wear an
electronic bracelet at the request of the man who's still her
husband. In reality, a judge is telling a little boy, my son,
who will one day be a man, that his mother is guilty, just
because his almighty father decided she was. Telling him
that she isn't really a mother because she isn't really a

woman because she doesn't really love men. Telling him that the law is always on the side of the most powerful and that freedom is nothing but a farce. To stay pure, I cross myself with lube, recite my credo wearing a jockstrap and confess wearing nipple clamps. The justice system is porn, love is porn, family is porn, the only thing that can never be porn is sex. Because it's the only time we shut up for once in our lives, the only time we stop lying.

12

They tell me not to publish the book, they tell me not to talk about girls, they tell me not to talk about fucking, they tell me I mustn't do anything to hurt Laurent, they tell me I mustn't shock the judges, they tell me to give myself a pen name, they tell me to let my hair grow, they tell me to become a lawyer again, they tell me to stop getting tattoos, they tell me to put on make-up, they ask if that's it now, no more guys, they tell me to try and talk to him, they tell me he might have taken things too far but it can't be easy for him, they tell me it's only normal for my son to push me away, they tell me a child needs a mother, they tell me a mother can't exist without her son, they tell me I must really be suffering, they tell me I don't know how you do it, they tell me, they tell me, they tell me.

13

A backdrop of water towers, regional train stations, abandoned football fields, a Lidl carpark, ugly concrete, patchy grass, the stinking, muddy banks of the Loire river, all of it bathed in a golden light. The taxi came to pick me up in Saint-Pierre-des-Corps, we drove past Camélinat stadium, the railway workers' estate, avenue Lénine, a bar called La Loco, we took route de la Levée, we drove along the Loire, the river was low, it was a gray day, we went past Leclerc, it has a McDonald's drive-thru now, we took the road up through the village, the driver dropped me off outside the house. My dad in front of the TV, the chimney full of ash, the nurse coming by to give him his Buprenorphine and whatever else he takes, the little bottles of Label 5 he buries at the bottom of the bin before I get there, the broken radiators, the cold tiles, the crumbling bathroom, the dust covering everything. Sometimes

I love Montlouis because of how ugly it is, sometimes I just hate it.

When I was a child, Montlouis was the house opposite, where my grandparents lived. The big house, we used to call it. There was the tennis court, the swimming pool, the raspberry and redcurrant bushes, the hunting lodges, the wooden garage for bikes, the Renault 4, the Renault 16, the lunches, the dinners, the small dining room, the large dining room, the bedrooms named after colors, the laundry room, the huge cupboard underneath the living room staircase with the wooden tennis rackets, some in their cases, some warped by time, the records, the old toys, the Jules Verne books in the library upstairs, Madame D., the maid who came in to clean in the morning and serve meals, limping because she had polio, speaking with a Belfort accent. My grandparents died, the house was sold, my dad doesn't have a cent to his name, for fifteen years he's been living on his own in the house where the cook used to live, he has no regrets. Before, he used to watch TV and smoke. Now he's hooked up to an oxygen tank all the time, he's quit.

I come to Montlouis to get away from everything. Me, my dad, each at the opposite end of the house, we hardly speak to each other, we don't sit at the table together, we bump into each other in the kitchen when we make our sandwiches and instant noodles, me putting a bit of ham inside a folded-up slice of white bread, him drowning his noodles in Tabasco. I come here to see him too, of course, even though I don't tell him that, even though we never talk about it. Two cats pretending to ignore each other, meeting in the middle of the night. You have to get used to this peculiar language, and whenever I bring girls over, even though I warn them, they're still a bit shocked, they still think we're crazy, and often they leave me soon after. But I think this is the way everyone should love. There are still a lot of Paul's things here, his bike, his room, his dress-up clothes, his toys. At first it felt like they belonged to a dead person, but now it's fine, I've gotten used to them.

I took out the big black leather satchel with my mom's book of modeling shots inside. I always used to think she looked too made up, too sexual in photos from before she was my mother, it made me a bit uncomfortable. I flick through the pages of the books and her beauty smacks me across the face. Her beauty and her power. I guess it would have taken strength to be around her, it would have taken guts, maybe my dad didn't always have it in him. I take out a photo, I show it to my dad and say, OK Dad, maybe your life right now, well . . . but look at her, not everyone can say they had someone like that in their life. Yes, he says. Then, I don't know why, but I say, It can't have been easy to love her. I feel him looking at me, stern. No, he says. He goes back to reading his book, I put the photos away. The good thing about opium, about heroin, is that when you're really into it, you don't want to fuck anymore, you can't even get hard, you don't give a shit. Why did he do drugs? G. asked me one day, much later. He did drugs because he did drugs.

He's probably the only one who really understands my grief, because we both have the same way of loving children, him and I. But whenever we talk about Paul, there's always a moment where he takes his head in his hands, gives me a strange look, and says, It can't be easy for Laurent. There's always a moment where it's Laurent he feels sorry for, Laurent he understands, where he becomes Laurent, where he suffers like Laurent. It does something visceral to them both, the fact that I'm sleeping with girls, I see it whenever I see my dad. My dad's body is Laurent's body. It's the same panic they experience. And suddenly my mind is flooded with all the images of my dad that I'd forgotten about because they're so different from everything he is. And in that moment, I remember that this gentle man, whom I've never seen angry, who's never jealous of anyone or anything, would sometimes hit my mother, my mother, who was the strength to his weakness. It didn't happen every day, but it happened, it did happen. I remember. Sometimes I wonder whether my son will struggle to be a man as much as his father does, as much as my father does.

The nurse knocks at the door, drops off a tumbler with his evening medication and sleeping tablets inside, then leaves. He takes them and goes to bed. Goodnight darling, goodnight, Dad. I watch him go, watch him walk down the corridor, it's starting to show, the fact that he's going to die, I wonder when, I wonder whether I should talk to him or whether I should just carry on acting as if he were already dead.

14

The guy at the swimming pool didn't believe me when I went to renew my three-month pass. He thought my birth date was off by a decade. Same thing happened the other day when I answered the Vieux Campeur satisfaction survey. They ticked the 25-35 box without asking me. It's always nice when that happens. Obviously I look a certain way, dress a certain way. But that doesn't explain everything. You gain ten years, easy, when you become gay. Everyone knows that. Dorian Gray effect guaranteed. I say this for the benefit of straight mothers everywhere. They're often quite depressed about aging. There's a simple solution. Just so they know. You could say that at twenty I was actually forty, and today I'm twenty. That's what people tell me. They say I'm living my teenage years now. I see what they mean. But I think it goes even beyond that. I'm turning time on its head. I'm taking a walk through it. Doing things ass-backwards. I'm messing with the fast-forward and rewind buttons. I'm in Back to the Future. I'm mixing all the ages up, switching from one to the next, choosing them at random, creating a signature cocktail, my very own recipe. It's the same with clothes, the same with gender, it depends on my mood or the situation. I've always thought adults were bad at acting like adults. With the girls I'm seeing, I've rediscovered the tomboy I was as a child. Long time no see. That's why it was strange going through all this with Paul by my side. Not because of my sex life. But because part of the new me is about revisiting my childhood, a time before he was born, establishing a connection to the me that existed before him, a me without him. It was like being ten or twelve years old and being his mother at the same time. Two different ages at once. Or all the ages. Or no age. That's what one of the girls told me once, You have no age. Nice. So maybe that's why gay people never seem to age. At least, not in the same way.

15

The children on my mom's side of the family weren't brought up by their parents, there were maids, nannies, the teacher who had her own room in the château, the English and Irish governesses who took care of the rest, good manners, affection, then around eight years old, the children were sent to boarding school. The boys were shipped off to the Jesuits, the girls went to the nuns, dressed either in navy blue outfits or in their uniforms. They were told it would make them stronger, it turned out to be true. They'd cry throughout the first term, then they got used to it. Their parents were still their parents, it was the nannies and the nuns who were forgotten about.

Maybe everything that's going on might make us hate each other less, you and me. Maybe it's one less thing to worry about, because it's already happened. Maybe we can love each other better now. The fight, the separation, I don't know what to call it because it wasn't really either of those things, there was no obvious cause, nobody really knows what happened. Maybe in time, we'll hate each other a little less. Sometimes, you just need to get somebody out of your life. You need to know it's possible. There's no other way.

I didn't need to go off into the woods, cover my tracks, go on the run. I didn't gun everyone down one night, set the house on fire, take the car then a train then a boat with the cops on my ass, the neighbors on TV saying none of it makes any sense, I looked normal, a little lonely maybe, but normal. The house, the dog, the kids, grandma, little wifey, the job, the holidays, the loans, the barbecue. Bang bang bang.

It suits me better this way. Of course it does. I like things to be clear. I don't want any misunderstandings. It suits me because I'm not done taking care of myself, the only thing I really care about, because it takes up a ton of time, and that's something you never have enough of, time. It suits me because love is terrifying. All types of love, even love for a child, maybe that's even the most terrifying of all. That's what I told the young one the other day. Just like I told the skinny one. Just like I told the others that came before and after them. Because they won't stop questioning me, because they don't understand, because they think I have a strange way of suffering, just like they think I have a strange way of loving. They tell me it scares them when I say it suits me having things just the way they are. The thing that scares me shitless is their fear. It makes me wonder what they want from me, what their vision of love is, whether they, too, can see into the abyss, the icy abyss of all the things there are to be afraid of.

16

Every day I go to Starbucks to write, I sit around in cafes, and I walk. I take my swimming bag, my cigarettes, a book, and just walk. No direction in particular. I prefer places that aren't too beautiful, I can't bear beauty anymore. It's cold and gray, one morning in November, Boulevard Arago. I don't even know what the hell I'm doing in the 13th. I reach a massive wall, I stop, I look up. La Santé prison. I'd forgotten about this place. I felt that same old rush, a mixture of pleasure and disgust. The same feeling in my stomach I always used to get, a slightly unhealthy feeling, whenever I would go to see my clients. The entrance, security check, the lawyer card, the token, the keys, taking the coins out of your pockets, taking your belt off so the detector doesn't beep, leaving your phone in the car or scooter, the yard, a corridor, a sort of welcome desk at the center of the quincunx, the doors with their bars, the guards, the smell of food, the fear, the sound of keys. It's dark inside, darker than Fresnes or Fleury. Section 1, section 2. Visiting room. The cells above. The men walking past, their sneakers, their joggers, their style, their virility. A small room, the small table, the crappy chairs, the light coming through the windows, the bars. The conversations, the case, the hearing, the next round of questioning, the next request for release. How long will it take, ma'am? I don't know. A long time.

17

In December, five months after the ruling in August, I finally saw the expert psychiatrist. The person who's supposed to tell the judge what to think. I saw Doctor A. in an office building near Gare de Lyon, an office he was probably paying a daily fee to rent because his own clinic was based somewhere in Aix, or Avignon, I always get them mixed up. I took a bus there, my scooter had been stolen but I didn't give a shit, I wasn't paying the insurance anymore anyway. He was a nice little man, the expert, he spoke with an accent from the south. He laughed. He said, Of course you love Paul, of course Paul loves you, of course you're not crazy, of course this of course that, he laughed and laughed, he said this kind of thing happens all the time. Though it's usually the other way round, it's usually the father who winds up having these kinds of problems, especially if he turns out to be a fag. He said he'd write up his report, of course, but it wouldn't make much difference. He said there wasn't much anyone could do now, if Laurent insisted on continuing this violence, this chaos he was creating for him and his son, he said it wouldn't be easy for Paul of course, living in a fishbowl, he shrugged his shoulders, he said I shouldn't give up, it could take years and even then, there's just no way of knowing.

18

I spent Christmas in Touraine, at my dad's. I showed up on the afternoon of the 24th, I went to Super U before it closed. I walked up and down the aisles, there were steaks and ostrich fillets in trays, turkeys, enormous things to feed twenty people, I didn't know what to buy. I got two beers, some foie gras because it's Christmas, some bread to make toast, probably some kind of ready-made dessert, I don't remember. We had dinner at eight o'clock, I gave him some presents, a perfume I stole from Bon Marché and the whole Dune saga with a yellow sticker on the front saying Gibert Jeune Special Offer. He said he was sorry he didn't get me anything, I said, Don't be silly, there's no need. He went to bed, I stayed up watching TV, I thought about all the people sitting around with their families, bored shitless, I felt lucky. I told myself there was nothing especially sad about the fact I wasn't with Paul, the fact that I hadn't spoken to him in almost a year, the fact that I didn't know where he was, that I wasn't able to call him or give him any gifts. It was my second Christmas without him. Did it make a difference whether or not it was Christmas? I hoped he wasn't thinking too much about it either. The cat that's always hanging around came to say hi. Merry Christmas, cat. The only pussy there is around here. I made a joke to lighten the mood.

19

Darling,

Don't listen to anyone who makes a big deal about us not seeing each other. Don't listen to anyone who says you must be missing me or tells you how sad you must be. Don't listen to anyone who gets uncomfortable when people talk about me or the situation or any of those things. I know you know you shouldn't listen to anyone else and that people say all kinds of things, you're pretty good at ignoring them, letting them say what they want.

The court case, the lies, the drama, I don't think there's much point talking to you about those things. You've seen for yourself what the justice system is, it doesn't take long to work out. And now you know what it looks like when love goes sour. It's good that you're learning. It isn't my fault if it's a little brutal. Life is brutal. Do you remember watching the bullfighting? How old were you then, six? Even then, people were looking at me like I was crazy taking you to see that. But I like bullfighting because it tells the truth. The truth about violence, fear, death. That's what makes it beautiful. We should celebrate the fact that it's possible to endure things. As for your dad and I, his anger towards me, everything he's said about me, to the judge, to you, don't take it to heart. Don't be angry with him. This kind of thing happens all the time, arguments between two people who once loved each other. That's the way it's always been, acid getting thrown in faces when people fall out of love. To be honest, I think it's much better than the people who have dinner together the day they get divorced. I prefer the truth of war over the hypocrisy of peace.

I don't know if you hate me. You don't have to answer. You're allowed to hate me. In fact, hate is a necessary part of love. There is no love without hate. Anyone who says otherwise is a liar or a coward. A child has to hate his parents, and above all, a son has to hate his mother. Yet so many sons aren't able to. Even a girl like me, who loved her mother like a son, even I don't know if I had it in me to hate her, and I think that's why she died, because she knew I would have never had the courage to kill her. She knew you must kill those you love, just to be sure you can do it, to remind yourself you always have the right. Love is nothing if not savage.

Don't be sad if you think of me, there's no use in being sad. But if you are sad, know that I think about you every day, I'm your mother, and that's something that will never change.

Love,
Mom.

(Letter never sent.)

20

Sometimes I can't remember his face, nor his voice. I wonder whether he's grown up, what he's like. It occurred to me when I went over to Apollonia's the other day, when I saw her sons. It's crazy how much they've grown in a year. I thought of Paul and how much he must have changed, too. A year and a half without him. Two Christmases, one of his birthdays, one Mother's Day, two of my birthdays. And all of the days in between. It's winter now, and since summer, since the ruling that said I'd be able to see him via the association, I haven't seen him at all, not even in a photo, I haven't heard his voice, not even on the phone. This is my second winter without him. What is this insane world I'm living in? This world where love is transformed into silence even without death? This world where things just cease to exist? This world where people tell me I'm the one who's insane when I point out the insanity? The proceedings are dragging out. The expert psychiatrist still hasn't filed his report, the association still doesn't have any spots free, Laurent still isn't answering me whenever I ask if I can see Paul for an hour in a cafe, at the cinema, at a friend's house. It wouldn't be so bad if I at least had something to hold on to. It's the not knowing that's unbearable, it's the time passing with no cutoff point, it's the lawyers, the judges, the experts, the association, it's the nausea, the fatigue. It's gotten to the point where I don't even know what I'm saying anymore, what I'm feeling, what I think, I don't even know who he is anymore, whether he still exists or whether he's just a string of sentences in my brain, something I've made up. This must be what madness is like.

It was cold that winter, I had no money, and I was sleeping with girls I didn't even like. By the time spring came around, I wanted to get away. I shoved my two pairs of jeans in a bag, left the keys to the 100ft^2 apartment at the cafe downstairs, sent an email to the owner. Turns out I didn't really need an apartment.

II

1

We've been seeing each other for about three months. We're having dinner in a little courtyard, the food's awful. She wants us to have a nice time, she wants me to tell her that I love her. In between apartments, I'm crashing at her place in Marcadet. I could have gone somewhere else, maybe stayed with some friends in Oberkampf, but having me there makes her happy because she wants to make believe, because I'm not giving her the love she wants. So now she's psyched about us shacking up together, even though it's only for three days, even though I leave as soon as she wakes up and often go out for dinner in the evenings, as if me sleeping in her bed and eating her yogurts made any difference, as if it meant anything at all, the days going by. I watch her counting them, piling them up like sugar cubes without ever resetting the counter to zero when I leave her, I wonder how many days she thinks it'll take for this fling to count as true love, I wonder how many days you can spend with someone you don't give a shit about, I wonder how long it takes for the hate to rear its ugly head. She cried this afternoon, she said she doesn't really understand where we're at, she feels like she can't talk to me anymore. I hold my hand up in the air, I say, I don't love you this much, then I lower it, I say, I don't love you this much, then I put my hand midway, I love you this much, that's how it is. I wait for her to leave me. I've already done it too many times.

2

One summer, one autumn, one winter. One association approved by the Paris Court of Appeal. Rue de Charenton. Family mediation. Meeting space. It was April by the time they finally called me, nine months after the ruling that said "unless the parties agree otherwise," I could exercise my visitation rights at the association while waiting for the second hearing, which I'll have to ask for once the expert psychiatrist files his report. The space is full of bright colors, children's furniture, crappy toys, the kind of forced cheerfulness you get in hospitals and prisons. I wait for them to call me. I'm not here to see my son, not yet, I'm here so I can meet them, the people at the association, as if I had anything to say to them, as if they had anything to teach me. In the waiting room, children I can't bear to look at, tired parents, the social services people. The place stinks of hardship, the real sort that poor people have to go through, the sort that never goes away. I think about my son, I don't want him to come here, I don't want him to see this world, he has no place here. I keep my jacket on, my headphones in my ears, I listen to rap because rap always protects you, I don't sit down. They can't get me, they'll never get me. Someone calls me inside. The director's there, a nice little lady about sixty years old who comes up to my chest, accompanied by a badly dressed intern. At five foot nine, standing there in my leather jacket, with my tattoos, my snobby accent, nose in the air, icy tone, I'm like a cross between the Baron de Charlus and Sid Vicious. I choose the raspberry red armchair. They sit down opposite me, on the teal sofa that sits a little lower. They talk about a "break in the story," "reestablishing the connection," they say "the mom" and "the dad." At first I hold back. I know I have to keep it together. But I can't help myself. I tell them I don't understand their vocabulary. I tell them I'm not his mom, I'm his mother, which is not the same thing at all. They said they'll be seeing Paul soon "with the dad," that they'll call me for the first meeting in a month or two. I leave. I light a cigarette. I breathe in, I breathe out. The anger disappears with the smoke.

3

In April, I move to the Marais, metro Arts-et-Métiers. I'm
getting to know lines 3 and 11. There's a Naturalia, a
Marché U, a café, a tobacconist. A guy I know said I could
take his brother's spare room, it's that kind of deal. We
agreed on six months. I buy him Whiskey, I pay the
cleaning lady. We don't cross paths much. I leave before
him in the morning, I always wake up early, I put on a pair
of jeans, I go to the Roi de Pique, I order a coffee, I read
a copy of Libération, I wait for him to leave for work, I go
back up. In the evenings I often go out for dinner, which
is a useless exercise because so does he. That's what I say to
myself every time I come back around midnight and he's
not there. If I'd have known he wasn't going to be there, I
wouldn't have blown twenty euros on some shitty terrace,
telling my life story to people I couldn't care less about.
During the day he's at work. Sometimes I see the cleaning

lady. She comes on Tuesdays and Fridays just before lunch. She always says, You are nice, Madame Constance. It reminds me of my childhood. She talks, she complains, I say, Yes, yes, I pick up my things and go swimming. I go to Les Halles. It's more expensive but the showers are big and so are the swimming lanes, plus it's always open. I walk there. Seven minutes, I counted. I like it when he goes away on the weekend. Sometimes I'm the one who goes away. To book fairs outside of Paris. I take trains, I stay in hotels. Sometimes I go to my dad's or one of the girls'. We usually manage to stay out of each other's way.

4

Right from the get-go there was a sexual tension between us. The moment I saw her, before we even spoke. Tall, blond, strong, blue eyes with the intensity of dark eyes, high-top Docs, short hair. A real butch, for a change. I figured she'd know what she was doing and she wouldn't be looking for love. She came to one of my readings. A lot of people came, we didn't get a chance to speak, I just caught her eye, but it was obvious. She knew my name, I didn't know hers, I figured she would find my email address, Facebook, Instagram, it wouldn't be that difficult. She wrote me the following day, she talked about my book, she addressed me as "vous." I addressed her as "tu," I asked her out for a drink, I told her to pick the place. We met on rue des Archives, at the Cactus, opposite the Cox. She ordered beer with Picon, I got a shandy, we talked a while, I looked at our glasses, we'd almost finished, I didn't want to order more, I counted to three, I kissed her, I said, Shall we go to yours? We took the metro, it was quite far, we had to change lines, we got out at Gambetta, I hadn't been there before, we got to hers, we started on the couch in the living room, we moved to the bedroom, it was pretty good, we talked a bit, we started again, she asked if I wanted to stay over, I said no.

I find the next one at Marché des Enfants Rouges, it's a nice day, she's wearing a sleeveless sweater, the skin on her shoulders is completely white, narrow, nervous face, short brown hair, blue eyes, she's a student, a pretty girl, a little shy, she tells me about growing up in the Tarn, the year she spent in London, she runs her hand through her short hair, she's a little awkward, she orders a drink, she tells me about her younger brother, she tells me about the pink color of her nipples, the fair hair on her cunt, she lights a cigarette, we go to her house, it's right next door.

The one after that tells me I'm intimidating. She smiles a lot. We stroke each other's bodies, we kiss on her couch. I wasn't paying attention when she gave the taxi driver her address. We went to get two beers from the corner shop. It must've been midnight. We'd already been drinking a while with some other people. When we finished our drinks, when everyone started saying so? and looking at their phones, I turned to her and said, Are we sleeping together or not? I know I can do that kind of thing now.

She puts some music on. The best thing for making love, she says. I can't remember what type of music, soul, I think. We talk a bit we fuck a bit we smoke a bit we sleep a bit. The next day she gets up before me, she goes to get croissants, she makes smoothies, there's even a jar of jam her mom made. I go outside, I look for a street sign, we're in the 18th, I go into a café, double espresso at the bar, BFMTV is playing, there's a copy of yesterday's *Le Parisien*. I take the metro, I don't have any battery, I go through the list, I update the figures, I sort them all by age, occupation, skin color, neighborhood, then put them all back: A metro map of conquests.

The next one can't be 25 yet, she looks a bit like Tanita Tikaram, she says she's slept with ninety girls, she's the same height as me. She says she's not looking for love. Anything but that. She says love is weakness. She's doing this for power. She doesn't want to be penetrated. Except maybe in the ass, occasionally. The day I met her, we went for a drink, she told me she never comes. We'd been speaking on Instagram. She made a joke. I sent her my address. She replied, When? I said, Now. I wanted to say tomorrow, the day after, because deep down I didn't give a shit about meeting, because it's exhausting, but I've learned that you have to want things, I've learned that you have to say now. I think she came, but I'm not sure, maybe she was faking it. She was pissed that I didn't have a dildo, she said she wanted to fuck me. She told me she felt like she'd been

(89)

shattered into a thousand pieces, complete chaos. She said she'd been doing a lot of coke. She said her thing was fucking guys in the ass, sucking them off, making them come, because she didn't want them inside her. It was chilly in the morning, she couldn't find her jacket, she was wearing denim shorts, a sky-blue shirt, black Nikes, she was cold, I gave her my gray hoodie, she had some coffee with sugar in it, she smoked a Marlboro, she called a taxi. She sent me a text later that day. She told me she didn't trust me but she liked me. She's gorgeous. But what's the point? We left it at that.

I don't flirt, I never flirt, I often say no and sometimes say yes. It doesn't really have anything to do with sex, let alone love. I'm starting to realize I can have just about anyone. You just need to have the guts, because everyone's so bored, everyone's waiting so desperately for something to happen.

The girl I had dinner with in the courtyard ended up leaving me. She kept crying all the time, she went through my things, she found one of my notebooks, she read my notes about girls, I met up with her in a cafe, everything went OK, she returned the notebook, I didn't apologize.

5

There's always someone with us. In case I stick my hand down his pants. In case I smack him. In case I start telling him about how I got eaten out and fucked at the same time while wearing nipple clamps this morning, slowly, very slowly, how many fingers, mommy? There's two of them. That's the procedure. It's that or nothing. One of them's an intern who talks too much, always telling us her life story. The other one's a thirty-year-old psychologist who's going to quit because she's sick of the association, she's looking for a job, an apartment, too. They never told me their last names, I don't remember their first names.

When the first meeting comes around in April, I don't want to go. I wonder what'll happen. I'm scared he's going to sulk. I'm scared I'm going to get hurt and I'm sick of getting hurt. And then I think about something else. I think about his body. His arms. His hands. His head. His hair. What's his hair like? Has it grown? I'm going to see him, I don't care if he sulks.

He smiles, he gives me a big hug, I haven't seen you for ages, Mom, he squeezes me for a few seconds, we don't say anything, then we sit down, we're still smiling when we start speaking, not too much though, we're feeling shy. Just pretend the nice little lady isn't there, forget about her, imagine she's a waitress in a cafe, I ask her for some water. He tells me lots of things, he talks and talks, he tells me all the fun things he's done since I last saw him, in school, out of school, the skiing badges, the sports he's doing. He saw my book in FNAC in the "top picks" section, the book with my face plastered across the front, he tells me he was with a friend and he said, That's my mom, he says he heard I was on TV, too. He's gotten so big, I say, I can't believe how tall you are, he says, We're all tall in the D. family, he presses his arm up against mine, he puts his hand on top of mine, he asks what I'm doing for the second week of school vacation, It's Easter soon, he says, It'd be nice to go to the sea, wouldn't it, Mom? Or we could go to Montlouis, is Grandpa all right? I hope those two morons from the association are taking notes. The association passes Paul's vacation request on to Laurent, Laurent refuses.

I always bring him something, cashew nuts, dates, raspberries, even little gifts, books, something from the Arsène Lupin series, Dumas' *Twenty Years After*, an Adidas T-shirt, a Velcro wallet, a compass keyring. Each time he says, Wow that's cool, he smiles, he hugs me, Thanks Mom, he touches my hand, he touches my arm, he leans against my shoulder.

Most of the time we're happy to see each other, even though it's like we're in a visiting room, it feels good to tell myself I'm not crazy, that I didn't dream up all the things I know about him, about us, he's there and so am I, just as we always have been, the procedure, the judges, the people, their opinions, it's all fake, it's all lies, delusions, the things people say can't change anything, what's real is real, it always will be.

But sometimes the hour drags. Sometimes we can't take any more. Sometimes I run out of things to say and so does he. Sometimes it feels grotesque, the way we exchange news, from afar, like bad actors, like two people who are no longer part of each other's lives. The cordial tone we put on when we have an audience. Sometimes that's all I can think about, how absurd it is to be speaking about nothing in front of these early childhood professionals who delight in our bond, who take notes on the progress we make, the stages we go through, the tiredness. Sometimes we get tired of reporting our schedules, talking about our activities, making plans that always fall through. Sometimes we just want to stop talking. Sometimes we just want to sleep. I can understand how this drives people to despair.

6

"Having homosexual relations cannot be considered a sign of mental instability in this day and age. Neither can writing books." The expert psychiatrist's report has come through. In April, nine months after the judge gave him six months to deliver it. That sentence was either in the introduction or the conclusion, I don't remember. The doctor deemed it necessary for an expert, a psychiatrist, to clarify this point, just in case there was any doubt in anyone's mind, Laurent's, the judges', five years after gay marriage was legalized. The law is the law, but if you look closer, it's falling apart at the seams. Apparently at the school, the school in the 6th district of Paris, there are parents who've said I'm sick. And hardly any of my family speaks to me anymore, apart from my dad, dearest papa, even if it wasn't easy at first.

In his report, the expert also recited some of the statements Paul had given when he saw him in December, before I got to meet him at the association. Things like "Dad keeps on asking me what she's doing. I want to make Dad happy. He wants me to tell him all the things Mom's doing. Every single thing. I tell him everything. She does a lot of things without my consent. Like one time she took me for lunch with her friends when I never said I wanted to go because I wanted to stay home and read. Dad told me to say that Mom never really took care of me. Dad told me to say that me and Mom don't do any activities together. Now I live with Dad and I have to see Mom at an association. I haven't seen her for six or seven months. I think she's strange, she's not normal, I don't know how to explain it. Dad earns way more money than Mom. He can buy me nice presents. Dad says Mom abandoned us. I want to only live with him because he's sad. I want to live with Dad and just see Mom sometimes. She doesn't look after me when I'm with her. She's on her computer writing her book all day long. Dad says it's not a normal book. She abandoned us to write her book and I don't think that's very good because now Dad is sad but I won't leave him."

Doctor A. concluded that "the minor is not speaking for himself here. He is criticizing his mother to avoid upsetting his father, with whom he lives on a daily basis. The mother has not exhibited signs of any psychiatric issues that could potentially cause Paul any harm. On the contrary, the mother has demonstrated that she is capable of giving Paul affection and more generally, everything a son needs from his mother. There are no psychiatric grounds to justify a legally enforced reduction of the mother's parental rights in relation to the father's."

The report's been delivered, but there's still no date for the hearing. There's no judge available to read it. My lawyer says, That's just the way it is. Maybe in a year. We'll see. The director of the association either doesn't know the report's been delivered or just doesn't give a shit. She says it's good that the bond is being reestablished. She feels useful. She thinks it's perfectly normal for us to be there. That's what she's there for, to help us, she's happy to see that things are going better. I ask her to read the report. She says she's swamped. She tells me to send it to her. She yelled at me when I told her I appealed. When I told her I didn't agree with the judge's ruling, she told me I was making a mistake, that there was no point being in denial.

7

I'm not a mother. Of course I'm not. Who would want to be? Apart from people who've failed at everything in life. People who have failed so hard at everything that having this status is the only way they've found to get back at the world. Some people seem to think that's how it works. Women who call themselves mothers because they have children. Men who call women mothers because they have children, all those dads with their cushy little lives. Or fathers who want to be mothers, like Laurent, to get back at women like me who aren't real women. "Mother" is worse than "woman." It's closer to servant. Or dog. But less fun. There's an element of malice. You only have to go on Instagram to see that. Or take a train and watch all the mothers fussing over their children, nagging them about every little thing, throwing their weight around and showing off that sadistic little bit of power they have, or think they have, as a mother, the humiliated becoming the humiliator, like the proletariat to the underclass. If people want to believe that women have a connection to the Moon, to nature, a special instinct that forces them to cling to motherhood and give up everything else, that's their business. But I'm not interested. There's no such thing as a mother. Mother as a status, an identity, a form of power, a lack of power, a position, dominated and dominant, victim and persecutor, it doesn't exist. None of these things exist. There's only love, which is completely different. Love that doesn't need love in return, love that doesn't ask for anything, love that knows what love is, love that never doubts, love that knows pain is nothing, that pain has nothing to do with it, that it's futile, that violence is always about the person inflicting it. My son knows all this. My son's a little mensch.

8

When it comes to love, nobody likes limits. When girls start to push it, I draw an imaginary line between them and me, and I tell them, My limit is Paul. That's what I said to A. when you were still staying with me every other week and me taking care of you was driving her mad. I said it to D., too, at Café Tournon, before I slept with her, when she said she'd need a lot of space and I told her that one day I'd get you back and then I wouldn't have the space she was asking me for anymore, the kind of space that takes over everything. But really it doesn't work like that, and now you've been gone so long I can't do it anymore.

You're always in my dreams. Before, the dreams were complicated, now the dreams are simple. Now we're all right. You're there, with me. And at the same time I have my life, these girls telling me they want to live with me. It's funny, all these dreams about love I'm having at the moment. Peaceful, serene dreams, not sexual ones, where there's no conflict between you-me and me-them, where it all works together. Of course, they're only dreams. And you're not really there, I guess. Apart from that one hour every fifteen days at the meeting space. But I think that's enough for me to be able to say that you're there. Because that's what I keep seeing. You're there and I'm there, even though we don't live together. I guess that's what's happening. I can't wait for us to get through this, to see each other normally. I can't wait, but I'm afraid, too. I'm afraid we won't be able to do it much longer.

I still worry about meeting you. About speaking to you. You have no idea how much I worry about it. I worry so much, I can't wait for it to be over. From start to finish. And you've no idea how relieved I feel on the weeks I don't see you. The other day, my roommate guessed right away that I'd seen you, because of how happy I was, we were talking, I said I'd seen you that afternoon and he said, Ah, that explains it! I thought about it, I think he's right. Even though I worry, I know everything's fine. And that changes everything. I know it's all right. I didn't dream it all up. It's the same me and you as it's always been. And frankly, nothing else matters. It's going to be OK, you know. Even if it's hard. I told you that, that I knew how hard it was. You smiled. When you come and hug me, it's not because you're sad, it's not you being gushy. It's just to make sure we're still here. Even when we're not together. I tell myself that's what the meeting space is for. So I'm telling you, too. And you reply, I know.

9

My goal is to have as little as possible. Things, places, people, lovers, my son, my friends. I thought that was partly what being gay was about. I thought dykes would be as cool as fags, always inventing new things. I was thinking of Edwige Belmore, Kathy Acker, Dorothy Allison, Nathalie Barney, even Beth Ditto. But I've been a victim of marketing. The girls I meet want an apartment, a dog, kids, they're in for a disappointment when they meet me. Son of a Bitch, it's written across my stomach, you find out as soon as you sleep with me, those are the terms of sale, honey. I've already done the whole mom and dad thing. Mom and mom is just as much of a drag. I have nothing against it, I'm not saying there's anything wrong with it, people can do whatever they want, whatever they're capable of, but personally it's not something I can do right now. As for being in a couple, I'm still in the

ICU. Sometimes I can't take any more of these girls. Wanting to hold hands, talking about their jobs, asking if we can go away for a weekend, a little holiday, to a nice restaurant. So what do you propose? They ask me. Nothing. Sometimes I hate them. Sometimes I wonder why I even bother sleeping with them. Half the time I'm not even that into them. A fuck is a fuck. People who fuck a lot aren't doing it for fun. I feel like a teenager in front of a PlayStation, giving myself brain damage from playing too much Call of Duty, a teenager that might just end up hanging himself in his room, killing half his class, or, just as likely, doing nothing at all. I wish I could've been a fag.

10

I leave the meeting space and decide to buy another copy of *Crazy for Vincent*. I threw mine out last year, along with all my other books. Because I was moving and you don't have space for books when your apartment is 100ft². But even before I threw everything out, I started to get rid of certain books: Guibert, Duvert, Belloc, Bataille, Dennis Cooper, Sade, Genet, I threw them all out because of Laurent's accusations, because of the court case. The judge said they were books, of course, they were just books. And yet here I am, going to a meeting space, talking to my son in front of people who take notes about us. I didn't do it the very same day, that would've been too emphatic, but on the following days, discreetly, casually, as if I were just gathering my things, I threw all those books out, I couldn't look at their covers, their titles. I wasn't guilty of anything, but what about them? I saw them in a different light, literature was a good scapegoat, the books had really fucked me over, even if it wasn't on purpose, even if it wasn't their fault, I was still mad at them. One morning, I took the lot of them, shoved them in a bag, went down the five flights of stairs and threw them in the trash.

11

The train leaves from Montparnasse in an hour. I've actually bought tickets, for once. It's May, the weather isn't great. I went swimming early, when the pool opened, to help me stay calm if anything goes wrong. I've been very careful not to get too excited. It was Paul who asked to go to Montlouis for a weekend. It's been almost a year and a half since we last spent a whole day together, since we last saw each other without an audience. Two years since he last saw my dad. They get on well. Paul always says, Isn't it funny how much I look like Grandpa? The association transmitted Paul's request, expressed in their presence during his hour with me, then reiterated in my absence, and Laurent finally said OK, seeing as he'd refused three times under various pretexts and was beginning, I think, to look like a moron. But then, one hour before we're supposed to leave, he calls me. He says Paul doesn't want to go anymore. He says he tried to insist but there's nothing he can do. He suggests we meet in a cafe, I accept. I tell myself it's a good sign, this cafe thing. Maybe he'll end up giving in. Not today, of course, but soon. This crusade of his must be exhausting. We haven't seen each other since the hearing. We haven't spoken normally to each other for a thousand years. We spent twenty years together, that's the first thing I see when he arrives, the past. He does too, I think. I can see he still loves me even though he hates me. We both say hi. He still wears the same clothes, loafers that cost a thousand euros, jeans a little on the tight side, those blue tailored shirts he has twenty of, the only thing he wears, and an old jacket, also tailored. Pretty chic in an uptight kind of way. He's losing his hair, he's gray in the face, tight-lipped. I guess he must be thinking about how I've aged, too, even though since I left him I've never felt younger. He says I smell good, asks me what perfume I'm wearing, how I am, whether I'm still swimming. Then without missing a beat he says I'm making no effort to resolve the situation. He says he has his sources. Then he says that Paul is doing really well, that he's getting excellent grades at school, that everything's been going well in his life since I left. The bells of Saint-Sulpice ring, then he says, All of us will wind up there in the end, anyway. That day, after I left him, as I was walking to the station to take the train alone, I thought about how everyone crosses paths with the devil at least once in life, because you have to experience evil, just like you have to experience love, desire, sadness. But the devil isn't a red monster with a fork in his hand, he's familiar, the most familiar thing of all, the devil doesn't have to be that frightening, he's as tall as me but not always as strong, a lost soul, a wretch. It's Paul I'm crying for.

12

Girls, girls, more girls. I'm upping the dose just to feel the same effect. A little blond cop, short hair, sexy, her badge on her belt, a gun, she gives me a look, I give her a look, we talk, she's on duty, I give her my number. A girl on a motorbike, I shout out to her as I'm crossing the road, she parks, comes over. A girl doing butterfly stroke, perfect body, I finish my length and give her a compliment, she comes to find me in the changing rooms. A trainee chef, shaved head, black double-breasted work jacket. A twenty-two-year-old Arab girl, bobbed hair, she tells me about her childhood in Hérault and her cousins in Grenoble, black clothes, white sneakers, nice skin. A fifty-year-old doctor who gets carried away, who wants to leave her husband, her children, but I leave her first. Like a convict counting the days, I check them off, I make lists, I draw up a tally on the wall.

13

Can we do a selfie, Mom? He's got a phone now. I can't
get him to give me his number. He says he doesn't know
it by heart, he says, I'll have to ask Dad, then he looks at
the floor. At the meeting space they say it shouldn't be
like this, at the meeting space they're beginning to understand. We talk about my dad, we talk about the
Weimaraner we used to have, we talk about a trip to Sicily
we went on two years ago for his eighth birthday, a few
months before the problems started, right before Laurent
took him and I couldn't see him anymore. I'd said to him,
Right, for your birthday, present or trip? He said trip.
We'd never really been away, at least never abroad, I
wanted him to see Italy. Off we went to Palermo, two
days in June, to the Grand Hotel et des Palmes where
Raymond Roussel killed himself, I spent the last of my
money, he was Tadzio, I was Silvana Mangano, what a

beautiful thing for a woman to have, a son. We went to the beach, we had granita, there was a street vendor shouting, Cocco bello, cocco bello! We laughed, we went inside the churches, we looked at the octopuses at the market, he danced in the street, spinning around in circles, his long arms spread out wide, singing, I watch the video on my phone now and then, it was great.

14

There's the one who likes coconut flavor Perle de Lait, the one who likes Kinder Schoko-bons and drinks beer, there's the one who uses Weleda creams, the one who drives a motorbike, the one who wears red lipstick, the one who wears football shorts, the one who does yoga, the ones who have kids, the ones who have dogs, the ones who have cats, the ones who have husbands, the ones who have a girlfriend, the ones who have a dad, the ones who have a shrink, the ones who have a hobby, the ones who like Sonic Youth, Dinu Lipatti, Black Flag, pills and electro, the ones who watch TV, the ones who go to the theater, the ones who smoke cigarettes, the ones who smoke weed, the ones who snort coke, the ones who are anorexic, the ones who are obsessed with food, the ones who sleep all morning, the insomniacs, the ones who yell, the ones who don't come, the ones who provide a running commentary, the ones who know, the ones who don't know, the ones who sleep naked, the ones who fall in love with me too fast, the ones who fall out of love without warning, the ones who dress me, the ones who undress me, the silent ones.

I like sex in the same way I like looking at people in the street, watching someone walk right in front of you without knowing them, the feeling of being so close and yet so distant. I like first times, one-night stands. I like first times because it doesn't have to be a good fuck, hardly anyone is good the first time, at least I'm not, because it doesn't matter, nothing matters the first time. I like first times because I like having sex with no strings attached, no reassurance, no obligations, no talks, no precedent, no familiarity. I like first times because they change your life without changing your life. I like the experience in itself. The innocence.

15

He draws a picture in my notebook, he signs his initials, he adds a D, he says, I think there should be a D because. He leaves the sentence hanging. I put my hand on his, I crouch down so I'm looking up at him, I say, It's going to be OK you know, it's going to be OK. He says, Yes, I know. We talk about something else. Then suddenly we're tired. We just want it to be over. We're exhausted from all the talking, talking in the way we're supposed to, playing the roles we have to play at the meeting space, we can't take any more. In one week, he'll be ten.

15

16

My friend Jibé and I call it exit 12, even though he's talking about boys. Exit 12 coming up, that's what we text each other when we start itching to break up, when love feels like an assault, when we've had enough. We tell each other to hold off for a minute, don't do it on an empty stomach, go for a swim, take a walk around the block, practice belly breathing. And then once it's done, we support each other, we congratulate each other, we comfort each other. We know what this says about us. We're not stupid. He and I understand one another without saying a word. I've done a lot of break-ups via text. Sometimes I meet up with them, when they're really invested, when there are things that need to be returned. I give as few reasons as possible, no real explanation. I try not to back down, try not to give in, I wait for it to be over, for them to get tired of talking. I've never been slapped, nobody's ever made a scene. It's afterwards that they get mad. That they start to hate me. That's when the texts come streaming in, the calls from an unknown number, the emails at 3:24 or 5:17 in the morning. What can I do about it if I don't like them anymore, if I don't want them anymore, what can I do, what can they do? Don't they feel it too, the stress, the problems, the niggling doubt, when they tell me they love me? Where's the violence inside them, where's that impulse, that side of life, of truth? I'm tired of myself, too, of course I am. Tired of falling apart so fast, so soon, tired of people, tired of things. Tired of relapsing every time, like a junkie looking for the next hit, two days later, two months, then waking up one morning feeling like I have a hangover. It can be exhausting, loving this way.

17

They're always talking about their parents, sometimes even before sex or breakfast. Do all girls do that? I'll have to ask my guy friends. I don't want the next one to tell me about her childhood, about her family, I want to find someone who doesn't care or has a different way of talking about it or at least waits a while before bringing it up. I want to find a girl who has something else to say, something else to tell me about herself.

18

This is no weather for fat people, says my roommate. It's almost summer, he's not getting any sleep either, I hear him come and go, sometimes there are voices, but usually he's alone. He smokes his Partagas no.4s in the living room, he takes showers, I hear the water running, three, four times each night, in the morning I see the bottles in the kitchen, the ashtrays, he says he needs to sleep, that he can't live like this, that he ought to work less, he says he already feels much better. Mornings are when I struggle to sleep, I've been waking up earlier and earlier, we're out of sync with our insomnias, I leave once the cafes and swimming pools open. Whenever we talk, a few words here and there, we tell each other we're doing well, that things keep getting better and better. He says he's thinking about buying an old Jag, an absolute bargain, he says he'll lend it to me if I want, he's worried, though, because there's no seatbelt in the back, he says that's the biggest risk for drivers, the passenger in the back seat could smash right into the back of your head, he's seen the statistics, there are loads of studies, he talks about them for hours. What did he mean by asking me to live with him, what does it mean to not be able to live alone, what's the meaning of his life, of mine? I don't mention it, neither does he.

When my hair's really short, the first few days after going to the hairdresser, I run my hand from the nape of my neck to my forehead, against the direction the hair is growing in, to feel my skull, my bones, my skeleton. Then it grows back and I stop running my hand across my head as much. I'd like to shave my head. I think about it every day. But maybe then there'll be nothing left to do. Maybe then I'll be out of ideas. Out of desires. That's the reason why I don't do it.

III

1

It's exhausting and refreshing all at once, not having a house, family, love, money. If Paul were still with me, I'd never have known. The cash flow situation has improved, incidentally. I got the money from the book. My life's getting back to normal. I've stopped stealing. Money's still a bit tight for my own apartment. But maybe it's for the best. What would I do with myself stuck between four walls? That's a tattoo prisoners get, a dot surrounded by four other dots, the prisoner in their cell. Apartments are fine as long as they're not mine, as long as I'm just passing through. None of that matters now that I know I can go from place to place, now that I've learned this about myself.

Sometimes I book a room in a hotel on the next street. So I can be alone. So I don't have to talk to anyone except room service. The first time I did it was when my roommate was hosting a dinner party. I didn't want to talk, didn't have the strength to laugh at drunk people's jokes. I've done it again since, not often, two, maybe three times, when I really couldn't take any more.

He's going to get tired of me not talking to him, avoiding him the way I do. He must think I'm strange or rude. I cared a lot about being polite when I was a child, but I'm over that now, too. Every time he asks if I want to have dinner together, I think it's because he wants to throw me out. But he doesn't. He takes me to a nice restaurant. He gets the bill. He says it's a pleasure. He asks if I'm writing. I thank him.

Summer's finally here. It's hot. He's away a lot of the time. I have the apartment to myself. I've met a girl, as well. We kept flirting. She was with someone. We ended up getting together. You have to be in love to stay in Paris for the summer.

2

I get up early, I close the bedroom door, I walk through the hallway, the living room. I make a coffee, I throw on a pair of pants, a shirt, I grab a nectarine, I leave a note, I take my bike, I go swimming. She's awake when I get back. She's on the sofa. Her hair's completely gray, her skin all matte, dark eyes, a cross between Jim Jarmusch and River Phoenix. She's wearing a black vest and my men's boxers. She's playing the guitar. There's one in my roommate's apartment. She plays Nick Cave and David Bowie, but a Bowie song I don't know, something about cologne and cool Canasta. I make more coffee and toast. I guess we talk a while. We go back to bed. Sex. Sometimes I think it's about desire, sometimes I think it's a reaction against something, but I don't know what. We fall asleep. The cleaning lady arrives, I hear the front door, she wants to come into my bedroom, she can see she's disturbing us, but she doesn't give a shit, we get dressed, I leave the room. The maid talks about the products I have to replace, she asks about my son, whom she doesn't know, she must realize it's complicated, or maybe someone's told her and she's talking about it just to piss me off, class revenge, she goes straight on to talk about her feet hurting, her retirement. I say to G., Let's get out of here. We go and sit in a cafe outside. Paris is empty, a little gray, it's hot. I knock my cup over, the coffee spills all over her pants. We might see each other later. We say goodbye. I leave her, she goes in the opposite direction, she turns the corner, I can't see her anymore, I start walking, then she appears again, she's come back. She says she's sad, she's scared. She's come back to tell me that. She's come back to cry, just for a moment, softly, on my shoulder. She says she's scared of the summer coming to an end. Or maybe she says she's scared of not making it to the end. Maybe she's crying because of the girl she left. Maybe it's because it's going too fast. Maybe it's something about love. She asks me if I understand. I say, Yes, no, I don't know.

République Magenta Stalingrad Laumière. Parts of Paris I never knew before. I like Stalingrad, I like the names of battles. I keep pedaling, the bike is light, it's a Peugeot, an old racing bike, 60 euros on leboncoin. One of the brakes conks out, I slow down, it's hot. The humidity, the Canal de l'Ourcq, I don't know this area. I know I've arrived when I see the sign "Sushi Paradise—20% off orders to go" opposite her house. Digicode, elevator, I put my bike in the kitchen, I go over to the big windows. There's a high-rise opposite, blocking the view on the left, but on the right there's just a huge stretch of sky, giving everything a sci-fi feel, Valerian vibes, almost utopian. We don't do much. I guess we talk a bit, open our books, listen to music. I'm sitting on the floor. I'm holding something in my hands. At some point she says, Come here, and we lie down. We sleep together but not right away. At first, we just lie there, our bodies pressed against one another. Then she rolls onto her stomach, she asks me to stroke her back, her ass. Then she stops talking, she doesn't tell me what to do like she sometimes does, like she did this morning, she lets me do what I want, she doesn't say a thing. Afterwards I lie close to her, one leg over her, I fall asleep. I wake up, she tells me not to go yet. Every time I leave, she says it feels like we'll never see each other again.

She does the paying, I do the driving. We've decided on Normandy. I say, It's nice around Bayeux. We buy food in plastic packaging at the service station. She chooses the music. I'm in love with your brother what's his name, the song goes. We find an Airbnb near Omaha beach. We go for a swim. We go for dinner. She beats me at ping pong. We get two rooms. No pressure to have sex. No pressure to be in love. In the morning she comes into my room. We have breakfast. We drive through the countryside. I take her to visit a cousin who lives in a château not

far away. It used to belong to my grandmother. There's
an ornamental lake with swans in it. We stay for twenty
minutes. We leave again. We fool around a bit in the
woodland, take the highway, she calls me Maurice, like
in the James Ivory film.

3

From the get-go, the deal is serious exclusive monogamy.
I say OK because I like her. I can see how it intensifies the
passion, how it increases the risk. The risk of breaking
your teeth, the few you have left, all in one go. The upside
is the simplicity.

4

Meanwhile Laurent was still doing exactly as he pleased. Except for one time in July, one year after the ruling, when Paul insisted. The two of us went to spend two days with my dad in Touraine. It'd been two years since we'd been able to do that, just be normal together, without doing anything in particular. Going shopping at the Super U, bike rides, hanging around at home, going fishing in the Loire, cooking, choosing a comic, telling him to go and take a bath, brush his teeth, Mom have you done spider patrol? I do spider patrol, I give him a hug, I come back to check on him once he's asleep, I slip the comic out of his hands, I put it on the bedside table, I pull the cover over him, I turn out the light, I go to bed, I read my book as if nothing had happened, as if everything were normal, I try not to smile too much.

In the train he says, We'll figure it out, Mom. We'll figure it out, darling. At Gare d'Austerlitz, Laurent's waiting on the platform, I say hi, I don't touch him, I say goodbye to Paul, I take the 5, I show up at G.'s. I smoke a cigarette on her balcony, I look at the high-rise, I think about how I'd like to live in a high-rise, in a district without any history.

A black plastic dildo, paraben free, made in USA, these are the best ones, she says, good quality leather for the strap, she gets down on her knees, I suck her rubber dick, I look up at her, she's beautiful, she's not smiling, she makes me turn over, she lies me flat on my stomach, she lifts me up a little, makes sure I'm at the right height, she slips a pillow underneath me, the click of the lid, the cold of the gel, I arch my back, she moves slowly, she's good at this, I can feel the surge, I come, I fall down flat on the pillow, it's nice to really get fucked, I needed love tonight.

5

I move back and forth between Paris and Touraine. I don't want to get too close, I don't want to move too fast, I don't want to wait around for her when she's not there. Around midday I take my bike, I go down to the river, I get overtaken by lorries, I pedal towards the campsite. There's an old swimming pool, open from June to September. The changing rooms are yellow and blue, the paint's peeling, like a holiday camp for boomers designed by the Front Populaire. It's lunch time, I'm the only one in the water. I chat with the brunette at the reception counter, she works as a dinner lady for the rest of the year, she's from Brittany, she misses the sea, but she's gotten used to it. I also talk to the swimming instructor, a cute girl with a tattoo on her ankle, she doesn't mind working over the summer, even though the days are long, when school starts up again, she has a job teaching kids to swim in Loches. She gives me some breathing exercises and tips for turning. She says you can only make progress by making mistakes, that's part of the process, otherwise you never get anywhere.

G. came to Montlouis that summer, too. She was on her way back from Italy. We FaceTimed one evening. She said it felt more real than texting, she wanted to see my face. The next day when I woke up, she told me she was on the train, that she'd be there in one hour. I told my dad, he said, Ah, very nice. I went to pick her up in the rental car. We spent the day alternating between my bedroom and the garden, we went to the vineyards in the evening, and spent the next day at the Loire. We swam, we fucked under the trees, like fags cruising, very Stranger by the Lake, it was fun and it was sexy. She doesn't seem fazed by me living like a vagabond, it doesn't shock her, it doesn't seem to scare her. She says it's love that scares her.

Later I take her to the station. Then I go to meet someone by Lidl to try out a 1997 Golf, 2000 euros, good condition. I tell myself I could come here more often if I had a car, if I could go swimming every day in Tours or Amboise when the campsite swimming pool is closed. Swimming to stay sane is even more necessary here than anywhere else. Montlouis makes you lose your mind. There's something in the air. Like the sirocco in *Death in*

Venice. But this isn't Venice and this isn't Dirk Bogarde, it's shitty Touraine and it's my dad. He's like a kind of antimatter, my dad, a negative force that absorbs everything, all *élan vital*, all desire, positive or negative, all joy, all anger. Thirty years the doctors have been saying he shouldn't still be alive, that nobody can survive with that level of toxins in their body, everything he's taken over the years and continues to take in some form or another. But the drugs are only a small part of it, the surface level, beneath that lies the obstinacy, the nothingness, the listlessness, the "no" he counters everything with. If we don't talk to each other, he and I, if I don't say anything to him, it's because there's nothing to say. *Vanitas vanitatum,* says his blank expression, every time you begin a sentence, every time you try to make a gesture. Thirty years and they're still surprised he's not dead. Thirty years and they're still saying he's an outlier. As if it were a competition. As if that were the only thing to be said on the matter. Tick tock tick tock. They don't get it at all. That's what's keeping him alive. Destroying the will of others. We all need a strength to live and that's his. Ninja strength, Dad. Thirty years, forty years, how long? How many years of killing everything off, refusing to die? And nobody can hate him, because he's such a charming man, my dad. He's the epitome of innocence, dirty, filthy innocence. Even from the other side of the house, he's contaminating me. If I were to stay one hour too long, I'd end up believing I'm just like him. Unable to tear myself away from anything. I'd end up believing it's in my blood, a law of nature. I'd end up believing we're all the same in this family. That we're the type of people you can't ever count on. It has nothing to do with love. There's a lot of love. But it's a listless kind of love that sits around, arms dangling by its sides. A desolate love. Sitting here watching each other sink into quicksand. Incapable of movement. The simplest of gestures. Or maybe it's just him, maybe he's the only one slowly killing us all off. First my mom. Then the others. I never feel guilty for not taking care of him. We love each other from a distance. If I got any closer, it'd cost me my life. Maybe my son's doing the same thing with me. Maybe he's just trying to save his own skin. Each time I see my dad, I get dangerously close to believing his bullshit. Poison, I tell you. I know it terrifies my sister, too. That's why she never wants to see me, why she never calls me, why I haven't heard from her once since I started having to deal with all this shit. In this family, even the slightest gesture is too much to ask.

I didn't buy the Golf. I liked the old car smell it had, but there was a problem with the gears, I had trouble getting it into fourth. I went back to Paris. I didn't see my son in August or September. I wonder when my dad will die. I'm not going to call him anymore.

6

At some point during the summer, having a roommate started to bother me, I can't stand him being home anymore, his presence makes me uncomfortable. In September, I decide to cast the net wide.

Studios, rooms, apartments, sofas, beds, I search left and right, left bank, right bank. But mostly right bank. The 3rd, the 4th, the 9th, the 11th, the 18th, the 19th. Before, I only knew the left bank, now I've broadened my horizons. I don't go to the 6th anymore, and I certainly don't go to the 5th, I don't even think about it. I stay in places two or three days, then I move on. I take my swimming things, my computer, a pair of jeans, two T-shirts, I travel light. I help myself to whatever's in the fridge, I share the kids' dinner, I bring croissants, I always eat standing up. I've become a nomad without crossing the périphérique, always on the run.

Sometimes I think I could take off, leave Paris. Because nothing's stopping me, no family, no job. Travel lighter. Really go away. Another city. Another climate. The sea. Or the road to nowhere. Hit the road, Jack. If only I had a car. But maybe it's best I don't, maybe I'd end up sleeping in it, never speaking to anyone, never needing anything again.

A studio. Abbesses. It doesn't get much light. But the weather's bad anyway. He's left clean sheets on the bed, two towels, like they do in hotels, and a joint. He's my friend's ex. This is where he stays when he doesn't have his kids. I'm taking advantage of other people's divorces. G. meets me at a bar in Pigalle, we have a drink, we go for dinner, we yell at each other for a bit. She says it's a terrible restaurant, the pasta sauce has been defrosted, it's still cold, she tells me to touch it with my finger. She stays over. The next day I wake up early, I go for a walk, I buy a bunch of crap for breakfast and the papers from a kiosk next to a carousel. I come home, we hang around, she's in a bad mood, so am I. She leaves, I watch TV like you do in a hotel, I fall asleep, it's nighttime when I wake up, I'm hungry, in the kitchenette there's some protein powder in tubs as big as buckets, he must be into body-building, I try the vanilla whey, it's good, I wonder whether I could stop eating food and live on shakes, never have to go shopping again. I do a Google search, check on forums for iron pumping addicts, the guys on there say it's not healthy, you have to carry on living a normal life.

I take the 12 to Sèvres-Babylone, I meet Marie at the Flore. I say hi to the cashier, then the manager, they say Paul's been in with his dad. We talk about kids, Marie says she'd like to have one, then later in life be like me "or Françoise Sagan," but we're not sure whether she had kids. Marie has four cars, three horses, two apartments, she earns her own money, she spends it the way we were taught to do in our fucked-up families, as if it had no value, as if there were no tomorrow, without ever being afraid, or at least without ever admitting it. It's the same thing with love. Do you think we're going to get through this? she asks. I say yes to make her happy. Things end up happening either way, even if it's tiring starting over all the time. She says, Do you think it's because your mom's dead? Do you think it's because my dad's dead? It's still raw for her, but it's been a long time since I thought about it. Still, neither of us can say whether we miss our parents, whether or not we're sad, whether we ever have been. Death doesn't faze me, even if it drives you mad when you think about all the things you keep surviving. She says the situation with Paul isn't a rehearsal, it's a way of preparing ourselves, because my mom died at my age. She takes me home in her car, her old Range Rover that smells of petrol, horses and the cigarettes we put out in the empty Coke cans.

I get home around 1 am. I've left my keys inside the studio. I slide my plastic swimming pass between the door and the frame, I must have done it twenty times, usually it works fine, not this time though. I climb up to the first floor, pulling myself up by the fingertips, I hoist myself over the balcony, I give the window a shove with my shoulder, it doesn't break, lucky again, I think. The next day I return the keys, I thank him for the weed, I don't tell him I didn't smoke it.

7

She keeps freaking out, she says it's not me, it's love. She says she's always like this at first, then it gets better, "once the relationship's more stable." She spoke to one of her friends who's some sort of shaman. He gave her a ritual. Every day for one month, she writes something on a piece of paper and drops it in a pot of honey. The pot's in the kitchen, not in plain view, but not hidden away either. I look at it one morning while I'm waiting for her to wake up, the ink hasn't faded yet, some parts are easy to read. There's no hate, scorn, boredom, nothing against me. She talks about herself, a pain in her heart, a pressure in her plexus, a tightening in her throat. One day she started shaking, she said she couldn't move. What's killing her? What can I do? She says it's her childhood that's haunting her. I say there's no such thing as childhood. Do you hear me? Look at me. There's no such thing.

8

Avenue Trudaine. Metro Barbès or Anvers. I move myself in amongst the Legos and the Pokémon cards. It's her youngest's bedroom, he'll sleep with his brother. I've known Apollonia for twenty years. We went to college together. She clinches deals, sits in meetings, closes sales. Her apartment's like a dentist's surgery with big, echoey rooms. She just divorced a guy who's younger than her, very good-looking, she gave him three kids then left him. It's not been easy, but that's life. When I meet people, we go to the cafe downstairs, they're open late, they sell cigarettes, and they have a terrace. In the morning I go out to buy fresh bread and croissants down the street, I see the Montparnasse tower on the horizon, there's something beautiful about it in the October light. It's mild out, everyone's saying it's not normal, talking about global warming. I like this heat, the end-of-the-world vibes, I don't care about the planet dying, I'm dying too, I think about *Tintin and The Shooting Star*, melting tarmac, the enormous moon that comes and crushes everything in *Melancholia*. I go swimming at the Georges Drigny pool in the street opposite. You need a euro to use the lockers, sometimes people forget to take their coins back and I keep them. I usually go at lunchtime while the kids are at school and Apollonia's at the office. Paul and I often used to go on vacation with them, to their village close to Ajaccio. He played with her boys, chasing lizards on the walls and catching frogs in a pond, swimming in the Mediterranean and in the river until his fingertips were all wrinkly. When can we see Paul? they ask. Soon, I say. I like them and I think they like me, too. Apollonia makes waffles in the morning and osso buco in the evening, she serves me Pontet-Canet, which I drink in the corner by the fire in a gray velvet armchair, warming my feet, I'm sleeping a bit better, I think I've even put on weight. The older boy is anxious. He always has been. Handsome and anxious. I went into his room this morning. Everyone had left, Apollonia and her two youngest, his classes didn't start until later, he's in seventh grade, his school's just across the road. I said, You know, I like it when you say we're all going to die and there's no point in anything. He looks at me without smiling, he says, You're lucky you're a girl, it's not easy being a boy. Apollonia's going to London for two days for work. I told her there was no need to call the babysitter, I'd go and pick the kids up from school, take care of the homework, bath time, dinner. This little family's doing me good.

I've been going more and more to G.'s, metro Crimée, Riquet or Laumière. She's given me her key, too. I've got more keys than a prison guard with all the apartments I'm squatting in. I keep them on the red carabiner she gave me, definitely a lesbian thing, she says. I hang it on a loop on the back of my jeans, I slip the keys into my back pocket, I look at myself in the mirror, she's right, it looks good.

She works during the week, we still see each other a lot, every weekend I stay at hers, too. Her anxiety has disappeared. She gives me her books to read, shows me her films, plays me her music, introduces me to her friends. I call her my sweetheart, she calls me her fiancée. We fuck a lot, of course, the months go by and still it's good, I'd even say it's getting better. When we walk down the street together, she says she feels like nothing bad can happen to her, that I'm like a guard dog protecting her.

I didn't tell my roommate I was moving out. I actually go round sometimes when he's not there. He lets me know when he's going away. That way me and G. don't always have to go to hers and I don't have to be hanging round avenue Trudaine all the time. It's my bachelor pad in the Marais. One day when he's not there, I'll go over, get my things, and leave the keys.

9

October, November, I'm wearing a Harrington jacket with a red tartan lining. He spotted it right away, he always notices what I'm wearing, my tattoos. He says the nicest one is the one on my left arm, the first one I got, the big one that goes from my elbow down to my wrist, the Caravaggio of the angel holding on to a falling man. He likes the little one on my right arm, too, the spaceship, After all, I was the one who drew it, he says. We were still living together when I got them. I haven't shown him the Son of a Bitch on my stomach, the one I got the summer the ruling was issued, in Montlouis, at the tattoo place opposite the deli, because I wanted to do something stupid, I needed to. Paul says the jacket's cool, I let him try it on because he's so big now, he's happy, I look at him and think, soon he'll be nabbing all my clothes. It's our first meeting since summer. I got an email in September with the new dates. Every other Saturday from 5pm–6pm, like a little hobby. At first, they proposed Sundays, but Sundays seemed too grim, I said I couldn't, I wouldn't be in Paris. Often, I go to meet G. afterwards, she waits for me in the neighborhood, at a bar she knows that does tapas and wine, I pretend I'm not sad, she pretends that's not the reason why she's there.

I get him the jacket as a present for the new school year. G. comes with me to a boutique on rue des Archives, she helps pick it out. It's the same one but different, navy blue with a green tartan lining, it's nice, too. Sometimes it feels strange that they don't know each other, I can even imagine them getting on well. I don't say anything to G. And I don't mention G. to Paul. Even if I'm dying to sometimes. The association would give me hell, Children don't need to know these things, about love, unless it's the love between a mom and a dad. When I'm there with him, I'm a plant with no soil, a paper cut-out, I don't have a life of my own. My whole world, everything I am, everything I do, he's completely cut off from.

He loves the jacket, he puts it on, he smiles, he wears it the whole time we're together, we take photos, with his phone, with mine, he talks about going back to school, he's in fifth grade, they call it year five at the private school he goes to. The 6th arrondissement, private schools, this is all new to the people at the meeting space. I've been thinking it'd be nice if things settled down a bit between the two of us by next year. That would be good timing for him. And for me. At some point, he takes a pen and my notebook on the table, he writes his initials, again he adds a D. The director of the association came to talk to me today before our meeting. She's beginning to understand, she says there's no reason for us to be here, she asks me to send the psychiatrist's report again, the report that says I'm normal, despite being a homosexual, despite having written a book. We still don't have a date for the hearing. She looks at the page in the notebook and she asks if she can take it to put in the dossier.

10

Often, when we kiss, she stops and looks at me, right up close, she scans my face with her dark eyes, she looks into each of my eyes in turn, first the right, then the left, then at my nose, then my mouth, then she starts over again. Sometimes I look back at her while she's examining me. I wonder whether it'll end like it always does, exchanging keys in a cafe, and when.

11

He's telling me about a girl he likes, he smiles when he talks about her, laughing almost, he sees her all the time, I don't know her, I ask him to describe her to me, he says, I don't know how to explain, she's a bit like you, he carries on smiling.

We look at photos on the computer. Photos of when he was little. Some of them I'm in. He says, It's weird seeing you with long hair. I ask him if he liked it better that way. No, the you now is the real you.

He wants to go back to Montlouis, it's autumn and the weather's still nice, we organize it, I let my father know, I buy the tickets, I tell Laurent the times, he cancels one hour beforehand, over the phone, that way there's less of a trail for the dossier. I'm tired of reliving the same old story, repeating the same sentences, saying the same things to friends when they ask me how my weekend was with Paul, whether things are working out with Paul, how things are going with Paul. It's not the events in themselves, it's the repetition that drives you crazy. I feel like a lab rat, carrying out the same task, at the same time, getting the same shock, with no solution. I don't know when we'll get a new date for the hearing. I don't even want to hope. I wonder whether he ever feels like throwing himself out the window, too, just to stop going round in circles, or whether that'll come later.

12

I wake up, I can't sleep any longer, often I go home in the middle of the night. I leave so I can read or try to sleep, I leave so I won't wake her up, I leave so I don't end up resenting her. And the next day I come back. Last night she asked me if I still wanted this, we've been seeing each other for six months now, she's happy with things now, she really wants to be with me now. What do you mean? I answered.

13

I've made a spreadsheet for the association, for the lawyer, for the judge. The dates of our meetings. The ones where he cooperated and the ones where he didn't. All the weekends Paul requested at the association that Laurent canceled either the night before or just before leaving. All the vacations. All the Wednesday afternoons. I spent a whole day going through Laurent's texts and emails, putting all of his hate into a single Excel file. This has been going on for almost two years. We might get a hearing after Christmas. Even the people at the association are saying that Paul and I should be able to see each other normally. That Laurent doesn't have any reason to be acting the way he is. The director's been leaving me messages, she says it's pathetic, she tells me to hang in there. In the beginning she said she wasn't worried, that Paul was fine, that she thought he seemed really strong, but since Laurent had put a stop to the visits at the association, since Paul got yelled at for asking if he could see me on Wednesdays and go to Montlouis one weekend per month, she says there might be a risk, that we might need to involve child protection, but she also says you never know what'll happen with child protection, that sometimes children can get placed in foster care, that you end up with them on your back until the child turns eighteen, she says it's best not to involve them, she says there's not a lot I can do.

14

I take the 4 from Barbès, change at Gare-de-l'Est, take the 7, get out at Riquet, and meet her at hers. We talk, we sit on her bed, the whole thing is stressing me out, I don't want to come, I just want to want you. I tell her that having kids is the mother of all bitches, it's like a fatal wound, it's worse than your parents dying or a relationship going down the drain, I tell her she was right not to have any. She tells me to calm down, she tells me not to be mad at her, she tells me he's just a child, she tells me everything will be OK. I'm wearing jeans, I don't have a T-shirt on, she draws two crosses over my nipples with her finger, she says that's what lesbians used to do in the '90s, they would go out topless with two Xs taped across their nipples, she says I'd look good like that, XX mother. I've shaved my head, it's starting to get cold, she says she'd like to meet him sometime, there's no rush.

15

I'm not asking for custody, not even joint custody. Just the right to see him and have him stay, every other weekend and half of school vacations. I'll be the traditional dad and he can be the traditional mom, dropping Paul off at school, picking him up from school, taking him to piano lessons, to music classes, to the swimming pool, taking him on vacation, living with him every day. What part of this nanny life suits him? What's the story he's telling himself? Every other weekend is the most I can ask for without causing disruption for Paul, they say. I have to take it slowly. Either way I don't have an apartment. Either way I'm used to this now.

16

Maybe it's the winter making us like this. She says she can't take any more. She says my life's difficult and so am I, she says she can't stand me being like this anymore, leaving at night, disappearing for days then coming back again, professing my love, she can't take it anymore, the back and forth, the hot and cold. She's had enough of my being a burden, enough of the wild child act. She's sick of my arrogance, the stupid things I say, going from one extreme to the other. She says one day she'll end up leaving me. I tell her she loves me too much to do that. She slaps me, I smile, it feels like a caress. I want her to hit me harder, I want her to tear my skin off, I can't take any more either.

17

We can do what we want, there's nobody on our backs, it almost feels strange, like we're doing something wrong. The association has extended my visitation rights. On Wednesdays, I go and pick him up from school at 12:30, after his drama class, and drop him off at 4:30 for his swimming lesson. At first Laurent said no, the director of the association insisted, there were discussions, in the end he gave in.

I'm waiting for Paul at the school, two years since I last set foot inside the place. Parents I normally say hi to pretend not to see me. Paul comes out, he's taller than the others, Hi Mom, he gives me a hug, he takes my hand, he says, So what are we doing? We say our ideas, Jardin des Plantes, bowling. I tell him I might have found an apartment, a studio near the school, just behind it. He says that'd be cool, he'll come for lunch. He asks me to call his dad, we call him, they speak for a moment. We take the line 4 from Vavin, we get out at Saint-Germain, we go to Azabu, the Japanese restaurant on rue Mazet, we used to come here when I had money, a treat for those halcyon days. I've reserved a table, he smiles, he squeezes my arm. We sit at the counter, we watch the guy making the food, a real Japanese guy who looks like a pirate with his bandana, we're sitting side by side, everything's going well, we're happy. Afterwards we're a bit short on time for bowling. I ask if he wants to rent some Limes, the electric scooters that have been all over Paris since the summer, we both think they're great, we're having a good time, sometimes I forget how much fun we have, him and me, then just like that I remember. Then it gets cold and we don't want to be outside anymore, we're a little tired, we go into Saint-Sulpice church, we still have half an hour. We take the holy water, we cross ourselves, we light a candle, we sit down, he gives me his hand, we speak in hushed voices, we rest. I take him to the swimming pool for his lesson, he says, It's a shame you don't have your swimsuit, you could have gone swimming in the next lane, I say, That's a good idea, next time I will. I give him a hug, Bye darling, Bye Mom, he goes into the changing rooms, he turns around, he says really loudly, Have a good week, Mom!

The following time, Laurent sends me an email two hours beforehand to cancel. And again the time after that. And again on Saturday at the association when we're supposed to be doing a debrief on how Wednesdays are going. The association emails him, he doesn't reply. It's because of the hearing. They've set the date for February. Laurent asked if Paul could provide a statement. I didn't find out until afterwards. Paul told the judge he didn't want to see me, that he never misses me. He didn't say I was crazy. It was better than the last time.

18

So of course she leaves me, she's gone before I can say Wait, before I can say Listen, before I can say Come back. I take the first train in the morning, I go all the way across France, I'm going to find out where she's disappeared to, where she's hiding, where she's gone to forget me, I see her, I talk to her, that's all I do, talk to her, I ask her to come back, I tell her I love her, I beg and plead, I say I'll do anything she wants, I ask her to forgive me, I make promises, I let her touch me, she brings her lips close to mine, kisses me, we get a hotel room, this time I pay, I let her take me to the shower and wash me the way you'd wash a corpse, she says, Come here, I fuck her, she comes, she leaves at midnight, she says she still loves me but she's leaving me, That's just the way it is. Sweetheart, heart breaker.

19

New pad, Denfert Rochereau, mezzanine, view over the rooftops. I've been here six months. I'm looking at the Polaroid on the wall. It's the only picture in the whole studio. A black and white photo. I took it one morning in summer. Paul's seven. He's sleeping in white boxers. He's thrown the covers off. The photo was taken from the side, his head's resting on the arm stretched out above his head, the other arm's under his chin, torso stretched out like a swimmer's. You can just make out his hip bone. His eyes are closed because he's sleeping. A happier photo wouldn't have felt right, and I like this one, he's asleep, he's not really with me.

The hearing finally came around. I won. Every other weekend. We'll see about vacations later, but at least it's something. The problem is that I have to pick him up from Laurent's.

The first time everything went well. It was winter. We took a Lime scooter to mine. He wanted to see where I lived. We stopped off at the Vietnamese, we got spring rolls and ginger beer. We went upstairs. I warned him it was small. He said it was really nice, he said, This is cozy, Mom. It reminded him of the apartment we lived in before because it had beams in it, because it had me in it. He said there was enough space for a poster on the wall, that he'd give me one if I wanted. I said it was his home too, that I'd give him a key. We ate at my desk then got a train to Montlouis, Montparnasse was close by. We arrived in the evening and left again the next day. We went on bike rides, we cooked, we played Uno, we read, we talked, talked about nothing, talked for the sake of it. We were together, it was nice. I left him to go and find his things, his toys, his books, his bed. We watched a politics show with my dad. There we were, the three of us, all looking the same, all talking the same, making the same comments about the TV, something languid in our tall bodies, something that comes back to me whenever I'm with them. I thought about everything I'd lost, everything that's irreparable. On the platform waiting to take the metro from Saint-Sulpice the next day, he stopped and said, Mom, can I have a hug? I took him in my arms. I thought about how he'd stop doing that in a year or so. When we got to Laurent's building, he said, You can just drop me off here. It's best if you don't come up because of Dad. He asked if we were seeing each other again in fifteen days. I said yes.

Fifteen days later, when I arrived at Laurent's place, Paul was still in bed in his pajamas. He wouldn't say a word, I couldn't get him out of bed, couldn't get him to talk to me, Laurent did nothing, I stayed there two hours, then I left. Laurent got his friends to come over as witnesses, to confirm that he had in fact opened the door to me, that he had said hello, that it was Paul who didn't want to come. I asked him if we could do things differently, if I could pick Paul up from school on Friday evenings rather than going over on Saturday mornings, he said no.

It went on like that all through winter and the beginning of spring. Sometimes he'd come with me, sometimes he wouldn't. There was no rhyme or reason to it. There was no way of knowing beforehand. No way of planning anything in advance. It was either a good day or a bad day. My stomach was in knots every other Saturday, just like when I was taking exams, just like when I was defending clients, I'd throw up before leaving the house.

When I couldn't get him to come with me, I'd go to the police to file a report. It was my lawyer who told me to do that, even though after doing it ten times I couldn't really see the point. I'd wait for hours. I'd waste my whole Saturday. The police were no strangers to this kind of situation. Often, the guy taking my statement would stop typing and tell me his own story. It was always the same. I'm starting to get used to it. We're one big family, those of us who walk out and end up losing our kids. They don't tell me everything's going to be OK. They know. That's something I realized recently. The cop in front of me is telling me that the justice system kills families. He says there comes a point where it's just too late, childhood goes by so fast.

When Paul did come, the time passed too quickly, and yet we didn't quite know what to do with ourselves, it was happy and sad at the same time. On the way home, when we were packing our things, when we were getting in the taxi or train, when we were making the same trip as the day before but in the opposite direction, we'd both slow down, talk less, stop smiling. On the train, he'd put his head on my shoulder, he'd fall asleep on me, sometimes I'd fall asleep too. When I got back, I went home, there was nobody waiting for me, I isolated myself, I waited for the sadness to subside, I waited for the depression to pass before going out, I wondered what the point of these weekends was, whether it was actually worse than not seeing him at all.

20

And then it stopped working altogether. I stopped going over to Laurent's. I stopped going to the cops. Now I send Paul texts, I have his number. Sometimes he replies, sometimes he doesn't. I'm getting better at crawl, I'm working on my breathing, holding my breath for 3, 5, 7 strokes, I'm working on my push offs, I can go for 12 meters, I have a lot more power now, I've even started doing butterfly, it opens up the lungs, you feel like you're flying. It's summer again and summer always agrees with me. It was yesterday, while I was riding my bike, that something dawned on me. I was coming home from Belleville, crossing Paris. I realized that the sadness was over. Not the kind of sadness that comes and goes, of course, but the kind that consumes you, that sadness has gone. I realized I'd finished grieving for my son. I said to myself, That's it now, the grieving's over. I felt good. I hadn't felt that good in years.

It came out of nowhere. Like when you wake up one day recovered from the flu. And when I thought about it, it'd been months since I last dreamt of him. I almost called the lawyer to say I didn't want anything anymore. Not even weekends or vacations. Then I realized there was no point even bothering because none of it was working anyway. There was nothing left to say. Nothing left to do. We barely see each other anymore. We have lunch together, once in a while. We don't know what to say to each other anymore. We're becoming strangers. Things are deteriorating. They're bound to. The memories from my life with him are fading. Or perhaps they're still there, but they don't knock the wind out of me like they used to. I can see other children without thinking about him. I think they're cute. It's not sad anymore. It doesn't feel like such a blow. Soon he'll be old enough to decide whether he wants to see me anymore at all. I'll let him do what he wants. Or maybe he'll get sick of his dad and want to move into my apartment with me. You never know with teenagers. And when I say my apartment, maybe it'll be our apartment, because we're talking about moving in together, S. and I. S. is the new one. We've been seeing each other for four months. It was when I decided to stop thinking about Paul all the time that things started moving forward with her. It's nice to have someone around who loves me. I've thought about it. There aren't that many different solutions.